PLAYLIST

Leave You Before You Love Me- Jonas Brothers/Marshmell0
Can't Help Falling In Love- Hailey Reinhart
Best Day Of My Life- Jesse McCartney
Fire on Fire- Sam Smith
If You Love Her- Forest Blakk/Meghan Trainor
Intro- Shawn Mendes
Rewrite The Stars- Zendaya/Zac Efron

CHAPTER ONE
Liam

"Daddy, do ya know what I learned today?" my daughter asks as I run the brush through her long, curly blonde locks. Thankfully, after five years of practice, I've almost mastered the art of brushing without tears, and I'd go out on a limb to say...braiding is my thing.

"Tell me, bug." I say, using her favorite nickname.

"A snail can sleep for three whole years! That's like, two years longer than my naps, I think."

Her blue eyes squint when a look of confusion passes over her face, and I can't help but laugh, "Oh? Where'd you learn that from?"

"At school. I'm not real sure about time, though. 'Cause five minutes sure feels like a long time when I haffta potty."

"You know, sometimes five minutes can feel like a long time. Like, when Daddy's coaching, and we need the winning goal, and it's right before the clock runs out. But then, five minutes can pass quicker than you can blink. That's what it feels like watching you and Ken grow up."

Ari looks at me, her sweet face a mask of seriousness, and lifts her little hand, complete with bright pink nail polish, to my cheek, "Don't worry, Daddy, I'll still love you when you're old."

Laughter erupts from my chest, and she quickly shushes me. I hold my hands up in surrender, mumbling, "Sorry."

"Anyone ever tell you that you're too young to act this old?"

"Nope," she says, letting the p pop.

"Well, I'm telling you, bug. You are too young to be so full of wisdom."

"What's Wiz-dom? Like Harry Potter? Wiz-ard?" Her bright eyes light up at the mention of one of her favorite movies.

"Not quite. It means…you're full of knowledge." I tap her curls, "Up here. Way smarter than most kids your age."

It shocks me sometimes that both of my girls are so damn smart. Sometimes, the things they say leave me questioning whether or not I'm smarter than a five-year-old.

"Now, time for bed. You've got school tomorrow, and Daddy's got a big day. Night, bug."

She climbs beneath the pink and purple comforter, snuggling with her stuffed unicorn, and I lean down and drop my lips against her forehead with a goodnight kiss.

"Love you, Daddy. The mostest."

"Never more than me."

It's our thing. They always say they love me "the mostest", and I always respond with "never more than me." Not a day goes by that I don't let these girls know that my love for them is never ending.

These are the moments that I feel like I finally got something right. When I look at both of them, with their blonde hair and blue eyes, they look like replicas of their mother. But inside? That's all

CLASSIFIEDS

the NEWSPAPER NANNY

MAREN MOORE

Copyright © 2021 by Maren Moore/R. Holmes
All rights reserved.
No part of this book may be reproduced in any form or by any electronic or mechanical means, including information storage and retrieval systems, without written permission from the authors, except for the use of brief quotations in a book review.
This is a work of fiction. Names, characters, places, businesses, companies, organizations, locales, events and incidents either are the product of the authors' imagination or used fictitiously. Any resemblances to actual persons, living or dead, is unintentional and co-incidental. The authors do not have any control over and do not assume any responsibility for authors' or third-party websites or their content.

Cover Design: R. Holmes
Formatting: Maren Moore

For Katie.
My plot fairy godmother.
I love you endlessly.
This one's for you.

THE NEWSPAPER NANNY

me. There isn't an ounce of their mother inside of them, and that's something I thank the heavens for.

I cut her light off, then I double-check that her unicorn night light is on and shut the door quietly behind me. Because Ari's older than Ken, I give her thirty more minutes to stay up, and trust me, she won't let me forget it.

And I never will. These girls taught me everything about love, life, and what it means to be a parent. How to be selfless and love something more than you could ever love yourself.

Becoming a single father to a two-month-old infant and a two-year-old was never in the plans, but somehow, together, just the three of us...we're making it.

When I feel like I have nothing left to give, I look at these girls and somehow put one foot in front of the other, and soon, it's our life. I'm still winging it half the time, and I'm definitely still mastering the art of tea time, baby dolls, and dress up high heels, but at the end of the day, I was made to be a father.

My girls and I can take on the world, and we don't need anyone else to do it.

Well, except now our lives are changing. A massive change that was completely unexpected but is necessary to keep this house and the lifestyle we've been used to.

Now, we *do* need someone.

A nanny.

Because I'm officially the Chicago Avalanche's head coach.

And regardless of what I want, the nanny is a necessity.

* * *

"I give up," I sigh, tossing the stack of resumes down onto my desk, which is already scattered with resume after resume. No matter who I find, I discover something I don't like about them. The fact of the matter is, everyone I've seen so far is not fit for this job.

What it all boils down to is that none of these people have the qualifications I need in someone I'm trusting with my girls. My girls are everything to me, so finding someone I can trust inexplicably is non-negotiable. With coaching, I'll be on the road six months out of the year, which means the nanny must be willing to devote her free time. *All* of her free time.

"Liam, you're being a tad…unreasonable," Reed, my best friend and the only person I *do* trust with the girls, says.

I sigh, "I'm not. This is a huge responsibility that I can't trust to just any person off the streets, Reed."

He looks at me incredulously before walking over and snatching a random resume off my desk and reading it out loud, "What about this one? She has a doctorate in early childhood development, dude. She knows how to play the piano. She speaks not one, but four languages."

I shake my head, knowing exactly which resume he's referring to, but he seems to have missed the reason that she's in the Absolutely Not pile. "She isn't CPR certified, and she has an allergy to vegetables, Reed. Literally, broccoli and carrot allergy. Two of the most important vegetables on the food pyramid. No, *hell* no."

"Okay, fine. Vegetable allergy, no. Got it." He picks up another resume, "This one sounds promising. Look."

He starts reading aloud again, "Wow, not only is she fluent in three languages, she is also a certified nutritionist AND has extensive knowledge of early childhood development."

Before he finishes, I'm already gathering the list in my head of why she is in the No pile.

"Nope. Don't like the vibe."

His eyebrows raise, "Oh, going on vibes now, are we? See, you're being unreasonable. Dude, you have to find someone, stat. Training camp starts in two weeks. That leaves you two weeks to find someone and get the girls accustomed to her before you leave."

I sigh exasperatedly. He's right, but it doesn't make it any easier. Every resume I've reviewed has yielded no results. Except one. But when she'd shown up for the interview, despite the stellar resume and recommendations, she'd been more interested in the fact that I was a professional hockey player, and now a coach.

And that's the last thing I want in someone who's going to be with my children full-time.

"Obviously you're getting nowhere with your unreasonable qualms in finding a nanny, but did you at least give Shana's friend a chance? The girl she was trying to hook you up with?"

My best friend is a playboy. No better way to put it. Takes one to know one, right? Well, that used to be my life. Before I'd married Carrie and had the girls. Now, I'd rather lose a limb than even think of rejoining the dating scene.

Not only do I have the girls to think about, but it's also a nightmare trying to decipher who is interested in *me* and who is interested in the ex-NHL player they googled. Nah, I have better shit to do.

Finding a woman is the last thing on my mind, and that isn't changing anytime soon.

"It's time, Liam. She's been gone for three years, and you're getting old."

"Thanks, dick. And no, I told her my schedule was hectic, but if it changed anytime soon, I'd give her a call."

He shakes his head, "You know, you don't have to be alone forever. You can find someone to spend your life with and stop punishing yourself for Carrie's mistakes. You deserve to be happy too, Liam."

"When did this conversation turn so deep? Shit. How about you find someone to settle down with and keep your dick out of the puck bunnies, hmm?"

"Ouch. I thought we were talking about you?" he asks. "Speaking of...I don't know if you wanna hear about this, but I think maybe you'd rather hear it from me, being your best friend and all, instead of reading it in the tabloids?"

My jaw tightens. Whatever it is, he's obviously worried about telling me. "Bad?"

He shrugs, "Guess it depends on your definition of *bad*. Could be just slightly uncomfortable. It's about...Carrie."

The last thing I want to discuss. Now...or ever.

"Hit me."

"Carrie's engaged. Some rookie from California. Heard it through the grapevine from somebody on the team."

His words should pierce something inside of me, like the thought of her had for so long, but now...Carrie is the last thing I'm worried about.

Abandoning your newborn and two-year-old because you no longer want to be a mother and have decided the retired hockey player life isn't your thing is something I will never—and I fucking mean *never*—look past. The truth is, the girls are better off without her. Not once in three years has she reached out. Called, texted, fucking emailed, sent a goddamn stork. It's like the girls never existed to her, and that shreds my damn heart.

Not for me, but for them.

Not that they ever really ask about her, but they will. One day, they'll have questions and wonder why their mother left them without so much as a backward glance.

When that time comes, I'll be transparent and honest because that's the kind of man I am—and the kind of father I will always be.

Until then, I'm going to love these girls with everything inside of me. I'm going to love them so much, so hard, that they never feel they are missing an ounce of love. That they never feel like they are missing *anything*.

We don't need anyone but us.

Except a nanny. We *need* a nanny.

"Carrie is none of my concern. I'm sure he can afford her lifestyle, and let's just hope he offers her something more enticing to stay than children."

Reed nods solemnly. She's a touchy subject in our house, but the last six months have been easier. Lighter. Even though she's been gone for three years, I've only come to terms with it in the past six months, after a few intensive therapy sessions. I've decided not to give her the hate she deserves because it's doing nothing but bringing me down with her. I'm focusing on my girls rather than the hate I once felt when her name was mentioned. And I know that hating her isn't going to make her be a mother. If the girls ever do want to know her one day, I don't want them to grow up in an unhealthy environment where she's involved.

"Right now, I'm worried about finding a nanny. Which seems

to be impossible, given my options."

I pick up the glass tumbler of scotch and drink it in a single gulp. I'm not much for drinking, but when Reed comes by, we share a scotch in my office and catch up on shit we've missed.

"Okay, have you tried everything?" he says, squinting.

"Everything I know to do. Except maybe put a damn ad in the classifieds, like it's the nineties again." I laugh.

"Wait, holy shit, that's a good idea. Put an ad in the paper. Seriously, do it. You don't even have to put your name, or anything personal besides your phone number or email. You could even make a fake email, so you don't have to give out yours."

"The newspaper? Reed, no one uses that shit anymore. I was fucking joking. Everything is online. Care.com, Indeed.com..."

"I know, but what if someone does? Some grandma who has a three-page resume and knows how to knit."

I drag a hand down my face, trying to think about what he's saying. A classified ad in the newspaper. The kind that you used to read over a bowl of cereal before you made it to the comic section when you were ten.

"What could it hurt?" he asks, shrugging before walking over and sitting in the leather chair opposite my desk. "Worth a shot. I mean...look at all of the options you have here, and you're being neurotic. This is my job as your bestie: to tell you when you're being over the top. Try it."

He pulls his phone out and starts typing away, then flips the screen around to show me, "Look, I created you an email."

I squint to read the words on his phone. DaddyISONanny@yahoo.com.

"Really, Reed?"

THE NEWSPAPER NANNY

Shrugging, he grins and types more, and seconds later, my phone pings, lighting up with a notification. He's sent me the email and log in.

"Try it, and if it fails, then you lose nothing. Who knows…You could find the best nanny out there."

"Fine."

What could it hurt? Anything is better than the stack of useless resumes in front of me.

MAREN MOORE

CHAPTER TWO

"Well, that was…underwhelming."

The understatement of a century. There are a lot of things I could be doing on a sunny Saturday afternoon, but really, there is no place I'd rather be than at Everwood Manor. The most…interesting nursing home in all of Chicago.

Nana scoffs, "I was expecting something more entertaining than that."

"Nana, he lost his dentures. I'd say that's pretty damn entertaining. They went flying across the room, look!" I laugh, my eyes never leaving Nana, and I see a smile tug at the corner of her thin lips. At eighty-four, she isn't a day over twenty-five in her mind—and hipper than I am on a bad day. Age never slowed her down. Well, not until recently, when she fell during disco night and broke her hip, which is what put her here, in Everwood.

"The first fist fight I've seen in twenty years, and all he does is knock him in the leg with a cane. How depressing. He could've at least punched him right in his fat nose," she grumbles.

"I'm sensing a bit of hostility here, Nana. Something you wanna tell me? Why are you holding a grudge against poor Mr. Reynolds?"

"Old geezer cheated at bingo last week."

I bite my lip to keep a straight face, "Oh? How does one actually *cheat* at bingo, Nan?"

Her gaze snaps to mine, "Don't sass me, Juliet Rose. His lying, cheating ass said he had numbers that he didn't. You see, I saw it with my own eyes. And just because I'm eighty doesn't mean I can't see."

"Well, Nana, I'm sorry that you didn't get to see a UFC version of a nursing home fist fight, but I love you, and I'll be back tomorrow." I stand from my seat next to her wheelchair and lean down to drop a kiss on her freshly permed hair.

"I love you too, my Juju. Don't forget my yarn please, darling."

As if I could ever. She'll call me at least two times before tomorrow to remind me.

"Oh, and what about some of those croissants from the bakery by your house? I've just been craving them so much, and since I'm now a prisoner of this old folks' home, do your Nana a solid and get some? Please?"

Her eyes twinkle, and I just shake my head and laugh.

This woman.

She knows I'd do anything for her, and she uses it to her advantage. Often.

"You got it, Nana. Love you."

I leave her sitting in the main room just as her best friends,

THE NEWSPAPER NANNY

Judith and Gladys, walk over and sit with her. At least she has them to keep her company. And boy, are those three a trio. I don't know how the staff handle them all together at once.

I don't get to visit her every day, depending on the shifts I pick up at the diner, and I worry that she'll get lonely, but knowing she's surrounded by them makes me feel slightly better about her having to stay here instead of her house, which we recently had to sell to pay off the mortgage.

With basically half a degree—aka, not having graduated—it seems like my options are limited when it comes to a job. It's like every job I've applied to either requires the degree or never returns my email or call after they find out I haven't actually graduated. But my savings are dwindling, and lately, I've been barely scraping by.

"Hi, Juliet," Andrea, the home's director, greets me as I walk by her office towards the exit. "Could you come see me for a moment?"

My gut sinks.

"Sure," I smile and walk into her office.

"Mind shutting that door?"

My stomach sinks even further, and before she even begins to speak, I know what this conversation will be about.

Andrea has truly been a godsend since Nana fell and I had to bring her here, going out of her way to make sure Nana was comfortable and calling me personally with updates when Nana had first arrived, which had soothed my anxiety about having to leave without her. It had been an adjustment for both of us. In her late fifties, with light hair that matches the soft brown of her eyes, Andrea is the kind of person you feel at ease around. Just her presence is calming, and it's the main reason I believe that she excels at her job.

When she smiles, it always reaches the corner of her eyes, crinkling in a way that brings comfort.

"I meant to call you earlier to discuss, but things have been so crazy here lately with Justine leaving and Maria on her maternity leave, I feel like I haven't gone home 'til midnight every night."

I take a seat in the leather chair opposite her and cross my legs, "I completely understand. If it's any consolation, you're doing a great job, Andrea. Everyone seems to be so happy and well taken care of. It's all anyone can hope for when searching for a place to trust with our loved ones."

Her eyes soften as she closes the ledger in front of her, "I appreciate that, sweetheart. I hate to have to have this conversation, but the home office is tightening the reins on our accounting."

And there it is. I've known it was coming, but I was hoping to stay in the bubble of denial just a bit longer.

I look down, tearing my gaze from hers so she doesn't see the tears well.

"Juliet, I know things are rough right now, and trust me, I am doing everything that I can to keep them off, but you're two months behind. They are no longer offering any leniency, and it doesn't matter whether I would go to bat for you or not. And I would—and do—you know that."

"I'm so sorry to put you in this position, Andrea. I'm trying to pick up extra shifts at the diner, but we're overstaffed, so it's been rough. I'm actively seeking a new job." I sniffle, brushing away the tears, "I promise, I will have the money soon and be completely caught up."

Andrea nods, her eyes full of sympathy, "I know, sweetheart,

THE NEWSPAPER NANNY

I just wanted to speak with you before the home office begins sending out letters. I didn't want you to be blindsided."

I nod.

"I'll keep you updated as I learn anything new, okay?"

"Thank you. I have to get home to get ready for work, but I will be back tomorrow."

She reaches out, taking my hand in hers, and for a moment, I feel like I might just fall apart right here in her office from the sheer kindness that she's offered. Or maybe it's the fact that I'm overwhelmed, with no light at the end of the tunnel.

"Thank you for everything, Andrea. It means the world to me. I appreciate it so much. I'll see you tomorrow."

She squeezes my hand and nods before letting go and letting me flee from her office.

The second I bust through the double doors at the exit, the tears I've been desperately holding back break free. I stifle the sob as I climb into my car.

"God," I cry, dropping my forehead to the steering wheel as I proceed to lose my shit in the parking lot of the nursing home.

When did things become such an absolute mess? Oh, what I wouldn't give to have Pops here with us now. He'd know exactly what to do.

I suck in a ragged breath and wipe the tears from my face.

You didn't come this far to give up. Get your shit together, Juliet. You are a bad ass bitch, and you've got this.

I shake my head and laugh, channeling my inner Nana and giving myself the pep talk of the century to clear the haze of the self-pity I'm wallowing in. This mantra will be the one to save me.

First things first: time to find a job. A better job. One that allows me to work around school so I can go back, get my degree and leave this hell hole. I bite my lip and pull my phone out, sending a quick text to my manager, Barb, that I won't be in today, then I toss my phone into the cup holder.

It's time to take control of my future.

Hours later, my hair is curled and my makeup is done to perfection—courtesy of my best friend, Alexandria—and I'm shoved into a pair of jeans so tight they're like a second skin, and I'm pretty sure I won't be able to breathe for the rest of the night.

"Why did I agree to letting you drag me out, again?" I groan as she tosses yet another shirt my way. To her favorite hole in the wall bar, Harry's, no less.

Huffing, Alex rolls her eyes and goes back to the mirror, where she checks her lip gloss again, for the twentieth time, "Because, Juliet Rose, you need a night out. As much as I love Nan and her golden girl squad, you are twenty-two and turning into an eighty-year-old more and more each day."

She walks over to where I'm still clutching the bright pink shirt and puts her hand on my shoulders, peering into my eyes. In six-inch heels, she towers over me, "Listen, it's one night out. One night isn't going to pause any of your grand plans. You can drink some tequila and hopefully meet a hot, single, muscle-y guy who makes you forget your responsibilities for five minutes. Think of it this way," she pauses, dabbing at her pink-tinted lip gloss on my lips, "Tonight can be a way to dive into the job hunt with a fresh, clear head, and you'll be relaxed and ready to take on the whole damn world."

"When you say it like that, it doesn't sound that bad."

"*That bad.*" She mimics, rolling her eyes, "Let's go, bitch. First shot's on me."

I throw the shirt on, tucking it into the waistband of my jeans and hurriedly lacing the faux Gucci belt through the loops. Alex is already ordering an Uber, so I grab my purse and quickly glance in the full-length mirror to check my appearance.

The jeans *do* make my ass look good, so I'll give her that.

And it *has* been so long since I've focused on anyone other than myself or Nana....

She's right.

A night out is *exactly* what I need.

The old Juliet is making a reappearance tonight, and Alex is right, maybe this is exactly what I need to jump into things with a fresh head.

"Oh God, this is the worst idea you've ever had, Alex—and you've had a lot of shit ideas. This might be worse than the time we drove two hours to see that guy you met on Tinder and found out he lived in his mom's basement."

The tequila burns as I swallow yet another shot, the lime and salt doing nothing to stop the fire as it slides down my throat.

"You're such a puss, Juliet. Bottoms up! And that idea wasn't that bad, he was just...more codependent than I was aware of."

I scoff, tossing my head back with a laugh, "Dude, his mom came down and asked if he wanted cookies."

She elbows my ribs and sticks out her tongue at my jest.

We've only been here for an hour, and I'll admit she was absolutely right. This is exactly what I needed, especially after the dreaded meeting with Andrea and both Nana's and my future on the line.

I need to close my eyes and not worry for five minutes, and that's exactly what I plan to do.

"Okay, enough tequila, or I might barf before midnight. Let's dance?" she cries over the music pounding through the speakers in the bar.

Harry's is the type of place you don't go unless you either A) have a death wish, or B) are Alexandria Warren.

Okay, maybe I'm exaggerating a bit, but seriously, it's not a place you'd pick out of a lineup because of its state-of-the-art amenities or great bar service.

But Alex knows the bartender, and he gives us shots for free most of the night.

The girl has connections everywhere, and I do mean *everywhere*.

Once, we went to an NBA player's birthday party, and I swear to God, I sat right next to Scott Disick. Alex was completely unfazed, but I had almost passed out on the floor to be rubbing elbows with people I'd only ever seen on the covers of magazines or on gossip sites.

So, some nights we ended up at over-the-top, celebrity-filled clubs, and other nights we ended up at Harry's. It had been a staple for the two of us while we were in college. A laid-back bar close to campus where we weren't likely to see the frat guys and football team.

"I fucking love this place." She grins and takes another sip of her IPA, which makes me squelch my nose in disgust.

"That crap is *nasty*," I tease, faking a gag. But I'm also one hundred percent serious at the same time. I don't know how she drinks it.

I'm more of a red bull and vodka or straight tequila kind of girl.

"It's an acquired taste. Tell me what's been going on? I feel like we haven't had a night out in forever. You're always so busy, Jules."

Alex is the only person on the face of the planet I allow to get away with that nickname. She's been calling me that since we were kids.

I sigh, picking at the edge of my napkin, before responding, "I'm behind on Nana's rent for the home. I've been picking up as many shifts as I can at the diner, but my boss is a complete piece of shit. Remember, I told you about him?"

She nods.

"Well, he is just such a creepy jerk. He's been cornering the girls at work, making them mop in front of him so he can watch them. Just an all-around asshole. He abuses his power and authority. I'm sick of it. But...if I don't pick up shifts, I'm going to lose my apartment, and then I don't know what's going to happen to Nana."

I bite my lip to keep the tears from falling. The taste of metal tinges my tongue, but I refuse to cry in the middle of a bar.

"Sorry," I whisper.

"Hey, don't you dare apologize for going through shit, Juliet. I'm your best friend, and best friends listen, no matter what."

She's right, but I still feel like I'm always throwing myself a pity party lately.

"Listen, bitch. As your best friend, it's my duty to tell you to pull yourself out of this funk and put your chin up. Hold that bitch high. You are a badass, and you never forget it."

I can't help but laugh. She's enthusiastic in a way I haven't felt in a long time.

"This is just a phase, babe. Start putting feelers out there, find you a better job than that diner with the creepy asshole, and then things will start looking up. You will be able to finish your last semester of school, enroll in your master's program, and become the most bad ass teacher there ever was."

My heart aches at the thought that I might actually not get to go back to school. When Pops got sick, I had to take off of school for a semester, and that was almost a year ago. Shortly after Nana fell and broke his hip after he passed and I had planned to only take one semester off, but one turned into two, and now I don't know when I'll be able to go back.

It's like a never-ending cycle. I need to graduate in order to use my degree to make more money. Three years of early childhood education, and I'm on my way to becoming a teacher and enrolling in the master's program to become a professor, but right now...I'm stuck.

"I'll ask around for you, okay?" Alex says, reaching out to grab my hand in hers.

"Thanks, Alex. I've been looking everywhere online and, hell, even reading the paper, but no one wants an "almost" teacher. That's how I feel lately—like my life is a series of almosts that never go anywhere."

"I say we drink. We forget about everything that's going on, and you give yourself one night of no stress, no worrying, and no responsibilities. It's going to work out exactly like it's supposed to, Juliet, I know it."

For mine and Nana's sakes, I hope she's right.

CHAPTER THREE
Liam

"Daddy, don't forget my Elsa backpack, pwease!" Kennedy cries exasperatedly from her car seat in the back of my SUV, just as I'm getting ready to pull out of the driveway and onto the highway.

Jesus. I forgot the backpack. How could I forget the backpack?

"Oh, right. One second."

Thrusting the door open, I hop down and sprint back to the house, pulling my keys out to unlock the door. Once inside, my eyes scour the house for the purple backpack that Ken can't possibly leave the house without.

Ah ha! Half pushed under the couch, next to Princess Sparkles, the fluffy, pale pink unicorn she sleeps with every night. I grab that, too, just in case—since I'm about five fucking seconds from being late for our first preseason practice and can't afford to come back for another forgotten toy.

It's fine. I've got this. Most of the time, doing the dad thing—carting around baby dolls, blankies, and every single thing Target owns for Elsa and Barbie—is no big deal, and I've grown so accustomed, I can do it with my eyes closed.

Today, on the other hand, has been a complete and utter shit show.

Meltdown after meltdown. One, because I wouldn't let her wear her nightgown, featuring Queen Elsa, per usual, out of the house. The next was Ari, who lost her shit because her pigtails weren't even. Which they were.

After the morning we've had, it solidifies my need for someone to help with the girls.

Fuck, I hate the thought of having to trust someone with them. The thought alone makes my chest tight, and panic runs rampant through my body, but I *need* this job.

Need, as in, I'll lose our house and the life the girls are accustomed to if I don't take the job.

Granted, it's a dream to become the coach of a hockey team you worshipped growing up. But change is fucking hard. Especially when your kids are involved.

Which is why they are coming to practice with me today to sit in the press box with a bag full of crayons, princess coloring books, and enough Barbies to last them a lifetime. Not common practice, but when you don't have any options, you make one. Even though this is my dream job, I'd been hesitant to take it because of what it means for the girls and our lifestyle. Not just the fact that I'll have to be away so much, but also that I'll now have to entertain the media far more than I'm comfortable with. I know it all comes with the job: the media, the paparazzi, the reporters desperate for a story of any kind. But the one thing I don't want is my kids in the public eye. I sure as fuck don't want them being followed by paparazzi and people thrusting cameras in their face. They're kids, for fuck's sake.

Back when I was a player, it was a constant. I'd felt like, no matter where I went, I was constantly being watched and followed, all for a photo or comment on the latest stats or scandals within the hockey world. Being a coach isn't as high profile as being a player, but it still puts me in front of a camera more than I would like. As much as I love hockey and need the job, I just don't want it to impact my girls.

I open the door to the SUV and slide back into the driver's seat, then I reach back to hand Ken her backpack, Princess Sparkles in tow.

"Here you go, baby girl."

She takes the backpack from my grip and gives me my favorite dimpled smile, "Tanks Daddy!"

Alright.

Girls - check

Princess Sparkles - check

Elsa backpack - check.

"Daddy, wait. You forgot to grab my hat!" Ari says, the second I throw the SUV in reverse.

Fuck. Fuck. Fuck.

They can't go to the rink without hats, scarf and jacket—house rule.

"Okay, Daddy'll be right back."

I climb out of the truck for the second time in five minutes and let myself back inside the house, heading straight to the coat rack for Ari's pink pompom beanie—and another scarf, for good measure. Because honestly, at this point, you can't have too much.

More is less in this case. Trust me.

I lock the house, sprint back to my car, and climb inside, slamming the door shut behind us. I turn to look at the girls, who are staring at me wide-eyed.

"What?" I ask.

They look at each other, then back at me, sharing a sister secret I'm not privy to.

"Breathe, Daddy. Remember what Aunt Shana taught you?" Ari says, sucking in a deep breath and exhaling using her hands for extra oomph.

Right.

My five-year-old is the next best thing to a therapist. She gets it from my sister, Shana, who is an actual licensed therapist. She spends half her time psychoanalyzing me, and Ari has overheard her once or twice. Now she thinks she's in charge of my mental health.

"Just running a bit behind, bug." I give her a smile, and she nods, still not convinced I'm not way more frazzled than I'm letting on.

Finally, after a longer than usual ride to the stadium, thanks to a traffic jam involving an overturned semi, we pull in my parking spot, and I begin unloading the girls and all of the stuff we've brought to keep them semi-occupied while I conduct my first practice as a coach.

No pressure.

"Alright, ladies, we've got the captain, Princess Sparkles, we've got the Elsa backpack, we've got coloring books, hats, scarfs, colors, Barbie and her village. Am I missing anything?"

A hat slips from my grip and onto the pavement, causing the girls to giggle.

"What's so funny?"

THE NEWSPAPER NANNY

Ari giggles louder, "You look funny, Daddy! You can't hold all that stuff."

Hell, don't I know it.

"Let's go, girls, and maybe, just maybe, I'll let you two put on your skates and skate after practice is done? Only if you're on your best behavior."

Their faces light up, and Ari nods, grabbing Kennedy's hand in hers and following behind me into the side door of the stadium.

One thing I've learned about parenting.

If all else fails, you break out the big guns.

Bribing.

"That's it! Move the fucking puck, Reed," I yell over the din of my players racing on the polished ice. We've been at this for two hours, preparing for the upcoming Allstar game and finally, it seems like they are working as a team, rather than against each other, like when they'd first stepped onto the ice.

Fucking finally.

The start of every season is rough. The guys are lazy, they've had rare time off to decompress and relax, and, while some jump back in head first, others take their time. Add in a new coach, and you're destined to get off to a rocky start.

Yeah, I know some of these guys from what I've seen on ESPN, or what had been carried down through the coaching staff. I know them from when I played hockey. But they don't know me, and I don't know how they run as a team. I don't know if Arriaga favors his right or left side when he takes a shot, or if McMullin is an aggressive player. Just like they don't know the type of coach I am—only what type of player I was.

There are bound to be bumps. Things we all have to learn about the others.

Reed skates up, hitting the side with force and tapping his stick along the wall, "What's up, *Coach*? Late today, huh?"

"Yeah, well…The girls are in the media box with Wilson's wife and her girls. Haven't found a nanny yet."

He shrugs, giving me an incredulous look, "Well if you weren't the pickiest motherfucker on the planet, and slightly overbearing and anal—"

"Fuck off. I'm still searching."

"Did you put the ad in the paper like we talked about?" he asks with his eyebrows raised.

No, because it's a ridiculous idea. No one reads the paper anymore. I don't have time to waste on something I know isn't going to help. I have no time to lose.

"Gonna take that as a no. Can't complain about it if you're not willing to exhaust all options, Coach."

He taps me lightly on the chest with his stick before grinning and skating off.

Mother fucker.

Nanny Needed

The ad I placed in the classified section of the Sunday paper is before me in big, bold letters.

I took Reed's advice and decided to give it a shot. Hell, he's right, what could it hurt?

And if I have any luck at all, it will be successful because, if I'm being honest, I'm fucking tired.

Finding someone you trust enough to move into your home and take care of your children is not easy. Especially since every applicant I've interviewed has *something* I can't look past.

Too qualified.

Not qualified enough.

The weird vegetable allergy.

The woman who let me know she'd be available for me at all *hours of the night before thrusting her tits at me.*

Honestly, did she think I was going to take her up on the offer, then give her the position to watch my *kids*?

Shaking my head, I run my hand through my hair, then lean back in my office chair.

It's late, way later than I should be up, since we've got practice tomorrow, but I've been refreshing my email, hoping an applicant worthy of my time comes through. The girls have been in bed for hours, and the house is quiet, with only the sound of a game I have playing in the background.

With preseason over and me heading on the road...I *have* to find a Nanny, and I *have* to do it now, rather than later.

I told myself when I took this job that I would keep hockey separate from my girls. Taking the girls with me on the road is not an option. I want stability and normalcy for them, not having to sleep in a different city every other night. And my only hope for ensuring they keep the normalcy that they need?

Finding a nanny.

CHAPTER FOUR
Juliet

It seems like fate that I've stumbled across this ad in the Sunday paper. Before Pops passed away, we had a tradition. Donuts and the Sunday paper. No matter what, Pops would show up every Sunday morning with a dozen donuts, six glazed and six chocolate with sprinkles, and we would sit together and read the paper. It was a tradition that carried on even once he was gone. One that always made me miss him terribly.

Some days, I brought the donuts and paper to Nana, and other days, I sat at my kitchen table, just like we'd done all those years ago.

So, when I stumbled across the ad that read:

Nanny Needed

Big and bold in the classifieds section, with a description that was exactly what I had been searching for, I decided it must be fate.

I smile because I know Pops had a hand in that up there. I just know it. The position checks all the boxes that I have for myself, and even though I've never been a "live-in" nanny before, the pay will be worth it. I'll no longer have to worry about the cost of keeping Nana at Everwood Manor. And, if I'm a live-in nanny, I'll no longer have to pay rent. It will take care of Nana's expenses, plus some, lifting an enormous weight off my shoulders.

It seems perfect.

Almost *too* perfect.

Which makes me nervous to send in a resume, but at this point, I have to take a chance.

I have to find a new job, and it has to be a job that will take care of Nana. The diner isn't cutting it any longer.

I open my email tab and start a new email before glancing back at the ad.

Wait, is the email...DaddyISONanny@me.com?

That's not exactly...professional? Certainly not on an ad that you would expect to see in the newspaper.

Weird.

Stop being judgmental, Juliet. Maybe he just has a sense of humor.

I hastily type in the email address, hoping this isn't a scam or some type of joke. I do it before the nagging voice inside of me makes me chicken out and change my mind.

To Whom It May Concern:

My name is Juliet, and I would love to apply for your nanny position. Based upon your ad, I feel that we are compatible. I'm currently on a hiatus but am enrolled at The University of Illinois and completing my senior year with a degree in Early Childhood Education.

THE NEWSPAPER NANNY

I am attaching my resume for reference and can provide additional references upon request. If you have any additional questions, please let me know, and I will be happy to answer them. I look forward to speaking with you soon.

Thank you for your consideration.

Juliet Michaels

I read through the message once, and then once again for good measure, checking for any errors or misspellings. Before I can change my mind, I click send and expel the breath that I had held in the entire time I typed the message.

There, it was done. And now...I wait.

"So, you applied for a job...that you found...in the newspaper?" Alex says, her voice laced with genuine confusion.

I laugh, "Yes, an *actual* newspaper. You know that was mine and Pop's tradition. I still read the paper on Sundays, and I just stumbled across it. It seems perfect, Alex. Like, so perfect I'm questioning whether or not the poster is a kidnapper trying to lure unsuspecting people like me."

I transfer the phone to my other ear as I open my laptop and refresh my email again. For the tenth time in the past fifteen minutes. Two days have passed, and I haven't received a response. Not surprising, given the luck I've had in the past few months with finding a position that works for my schedule with Nana, pays enough to keep her taken care of and me not having to eat ramen noodles nightly, and that I think I could genuinely be happy at.

But it doesn't stop me from checking my messages an alarming number of times on the off chance that I get a response.

Every time I'm passed up for a job or don't get an email or call back, I feel my hope diminishing. I have three years of college towards a degree I haven't yet secured, and I'm beginning to think that it's pointless to continue searching.

"Uh, yeah. Not sure that you should go alone, Jules. What if they kidnap you and keep you in their basement?"

"I highly doubt a kidnapper is actually going to put an ad in the Sunday paper, Alex. But I also highly doubt I'll get a response, anyway. Listen, I'll text you later. I'm picking up a shift at the diner, and I'm about to walk out the door."

She huffs, "I can't wait until you can leave the diner behind. Love you."

"Love you more."

We end the call, and I tuck my phone in the back pocket of my skirt. The uniform they require us to wear is ridiculously hideous, but I do my best to look halfway decent. I always put my hair in a low bun, off my neck and out of my face, since some nights I barely have time to stop and breathe. Sometimes, I wear makeup, but other nights I throw on some tinted moisturizer and lip balm and call it a day.

It's not like I have anyone to impress, anyway. My love life is as nonexistent as my career.

By the time I leave the house and make it to the diner, I'm running five minutes late. I open the front door and rush inside, tying my apron just as the door shuts behind me.

"Juliet...you're late," Gary, the manager says, looking down his nose with disapproval at me.

Gary, the asshole with the God complex.

Not only is he possibly the biggest douchebag on the planet, but he also has zero fashion sense. Like, every day, he's dressed in high water slacks and mismatched ties, but somehow, he still thinks he's the hottest thing since Paul Walker.

I can't even begin to understand the logic on this one. And my patience with Gary is slowly ticking away inside of me like a bomb. He's inappropriate with the girls who work here, and I've intervened several times when he's been inappropriate with them. So now, he takes it out on me by being the ultimate hard ass.

Prick.

"Sorry Gary, it won't happen again."

His thin lips flatten even more in a not amused look before he shakes his head, "You know, Juliet, you've been late four times this month. Four. Times." He holds up my punch card like I don't already know what time I've gotten here.

Breathe, Juliet. You need this job until you find another one. For the foreseeable future, you'll be stuck at Easyup Diner, dealing with Gary and the unbelievably shitty pay.

I suck in a breath before responding, "I'm sorry. I have a lot going on with my Nana. I know that isn't an excuse. I promise I will be on time going forward, Gary."

I give him a bright smile, hoping to appease him for the time being.

"Can I see you in my office, please?" He doesn't wait for my answer; he simply turns and walks away.

Great. Today is going to be just great.

I gather my composure and follow him to his office. Once I'm inside, he tries to shut the door, but I put my hand up.

"I would prefer if you left the door open, please."

His eyes narrow, "Do I make you uncomfortable?"

The audacity of this prick.

Of fucking course you do. After all the times I've seen him touch the other girls without their permission, I wouldn't put anything past him.

"Shutting the door is unnecessary. Whatever you need to say, you can say it to me with the door open. If that's an issue, I would be happy to speak with the owner about it."

"Fine." He sits in the old, busted leather chair behind his desk, which looks to be on its last leg.

If he wasn't such a complete ass, I would almost feel sorry for him. He's pushing forty, with thinning hair and a beer gut, and I'm pretty sure he still lives at home with his mother. I've seen her pick him up and drop him off on occasion. Obviously, he's not the ambitious type.

"Unfortunately, Juliet, if you're late again, I'm going to have to let you go." He pauses, looking for a reaction from me. One that he will not get. "Listen, I've been extremely understanding of your situation. You've called in to take care of your Nana, which I can appreciate—the fact that you work so hard for her."

"Gary, I've called in once in the last six months. And it was because she fell and broke her hip, and I had to care for her after surgery." I fold my arms across my chest. Is he serious right now?

"Still, you've called in, you've been late numerous times, and honestly I don't appreciate your attitude towards me."

It takes everything inside me not to let my jaw hit the floor in shock.

My attitude towards *him*?

"I'm sorry?" I sputter. I'm completely flabbergasted.

He shrugs, and a grin spreads across his face, making him look even more like the creep he truly is, "But I'm a compassionate guy. I believe that everyone deserves a second chance. I'm sure there's something we can come to an agreement on to rectify the situation?"

The way his beady eyes slither down my body in a less than subtle way makes me shiver with disgust.

"I truly hope you aren't stupid enough to try and...blackmail me into sleeping with you, Gary? Because I hope you know that I would rather be jobless and living on the side of the street than ever touch you," I spit.

I'm so angry, so absolutely disgusted at his blatant disrespect.

"I—I—that's.... I did—"

I put my hand up, stopping him.

"Let's get one thing straight, Gary." His name rolls off my tongue like acid, "You may be my boss. You might have power I do not have, but understand one thing. If you so much as *look* in my direction again with *anything* but respect and professionalism, I will walk out of this diner and straight to WBML, and I will let them know how you have preyed on so many young girls working at this diner. Abusing your power for your own sick, personal gain."

Suddenly, his face goes as white as the grease-stained button up he's wearing. He swallows visibly.

"And if you ever, and I mean ever, touch another female without her permission again, I will *ruin* you."

With that, I turn on my heel, slam his rickety door shut behind me, and head straight to the kitchen.

The second I push through the door, Tommy, Mario, and Isabella scatter to avoid falling over. Busted with their ears against the door.

If I wasn't so shaken, I would laugh. But I am shaking so hard my teeth chatter.

I'm enraged. It's men like Gary who are the problem in today's world. He's made this such a toxic work environment. I want to report him anyway, but without proof, I'm not sure the owner would take my claims seriously. Maybe the other girls will come forward. Although, I doubt it, since they are in the same position as me. Desperate for work, and nowhere to go to.

Isabella walks over and gathers me in her arms in a hug that is so comforting, I feel the tears well in my eyes. I'm emotionally spent.

"He is such a piece of shit. You sure told his ass, Michaels. I am proud," she whispers.

Isa is a big part of why I stay at the diner, besides the fact that I need this job, badly. She's like the mother I never had. In her late fifties, she has dark hair and kind eyes, and she can cuss Gary like a dog in Spanish and he has no idea what is happening. She has become so much more than a coworker in my time here. She's family.

When we have free time, she shows me photos of her grandchildren, and we talk about how much she loves being their abuela. On her off days, she spends her time in her kitchen, and each time I come in to work, her famous homemade tamales are in the fridge with my name on them.

And that's what matters. Family. Not Gary and his slimy, disgusting self.

"Are you okay?"

She pulls back to look at me, and I nod, sucking in a calming breath.

"I'm okay. He deserved a kick right to the nuts, but I have to stay out of jail for assault because I don't have the money to pay bond." I laugh, then swipe away a stray tear that's fallen. "I just... I'm so angry. He was so degrading. I shouldn't be surprised, but I just never expected him to bring me in there and proposition me like that."

"Want me to kick his ass?" Tommy asks. He's back behind the grill, flipping rows of burgers with the oversized spatula, but his gaze is full of concern as he stares at me.

"No, Tommy. You need this job, too. We just have to suck it up and deal with it for now, as much as it sucks and I hate it. Hopefully, he takes my threat seriously."

Tommy nods, and Isabella sighs.

We're all tired of his shit. But he preys on people like us: the ones stuck in shitty situations with no other options, knowing that we can't just leave.

I dry the tears and take a second in the bathroom to try and shake off what happened, but the rest of the night is ruined.

For a Thursday night, we're surprisingly completely dead. Only three customers come in, and only one of them tips. If I wasn't closing tonight, I would have already been cut, but I am here 'til we are locked up. Since we're completely dead, I sit at a booth close to the kitchen and pull my phone out.

I'll check my emails and maybe read a few pages on my kindle app, since my side work is done.

I look around for Gary and, thankfully, he's nowhere to be

seen. The diner is completely deserted, except for Tommy, who's in the kitchen working over the grill.

My phone is so slow, it takes a full three minutes to update, but when it finally does, there's an email in the inbox from DaddyISONanny. If it weren't for the fact that Gary might fire me, I'd scream.

Calm down, Juliet.

He could be rejecting me, for all I know, with the excuse that he's gone a different route. The same response I've received a hundred times in the past few months.

Don't get your hopes up and then be disappointed.

I shakily open the message, holding my breath as my eyes scan the text.

Dear Juliet,

Thank you for your interest. I appreciate your response to my ad.

The position available is one I would prefer to discuss in person, as I wouldn't like to waste either your time or mine, which I'm sure you can understand.

I do have a few additional questions.

1. Do you have any food allergies?

2. Do you know how to braid hair?

With that being said, please understand that this position is for a live-in nanny, and it is not an opportunity to proposition me for a date. There seems to have been some confusion with my previous applicants, so I would like to clear that up.

Thank you for your prompt response.

I read the last paragraph twice because, surely, I've misread it. Proposition him for a date? What. The. Hell.

THE NEWSPAPER NANNY

There seems to have been some confusion with my previous applicants, so I would like to clear that up.

Does that mean that the last person he interviewed tried to... flirt with him? At an interview?

Wow.

I don't know what to think of his response. His questions are random, and the dating part has completely confused me. Of all questions to ask, those are the ones he asks?

Out of habit, I chew the side of my cheek in thought, and I don't even hear the bell above the door jingle as it opens. I'm so lost in my own world, rereading the stupid, insanely random email, that I don't even notice him until he's standing next to my table, clearing his throat.

"Excuse me?"

When I look up, I'm not expecting the most attractive man I've ever seen to be standing only a few feet from me. I scramble from the booth, trying to smooth the apron and skirt as I do, and my phone goes flying. It skids across the floor, coming to a stop with a thud as it hits a barstool at the bar.

Oh God.

"I'm so sorry," I apologize profusely as I bend down to get my phone.

It would happen that he bends down to pick it up at the same exact time, and in the process, we bump our heads together in a clumsy fumble.

"Shit," I curse.

"Fuck," he mutters.

Our words run together.

Wincing, I rub my head and pray that my face isn't as red as the sign on the wall. This is so embarrassing. I'm mortified.

"Oh God, I'm so sorry. God, I'm such a klutz."

Sexy Stranger, as I've dubbed him, smiles, even though it's more of a grimace as he clutches his nose, which must be what I hit.

"No problem." His voice is pure velvet, dripping in seduction. Is that even a thing? A low, growly timbre that I can feel somewhere deep inside my stomach.

When he pulls his hand away, blood drips from his nose, and I almost faint on the spot. Just when I'd thought things couldn't get any worse, I bust the sexiest man alive's nose with my clumsiness.

Great, Juliet.

The icing on the cake of an already shit night.

"Oh God," I cry, dashing for napkins.

"I'm fine. It's fine," he mumbles, holding his nose, but the blood drips past onto his hand.

"You're bleeding everywhere. I'm so sorry. Please sit here, and I'll go grab some clean rags from the back."

He doesn't argue and sinks into the booth seat. I almost trip when I turn to run to the back, but I make it to the back unscathed and grab an entire stack of rags from the box. Never in my life have I been as thankful as I am right now that Gary is capable of doing one thing, literally only *one* thing right, and that's keeping the back stocked. The rags are brand new.

I run back to the booth and thrust the rags at him, which he takes and presses to his nose. The stark, red blood bleeds through the bright white rag, but it seems to be slowing.

"I cannot apologize enough. You came here for dinner and got a busted nose in the process. Please, let me buy your dinner."

SS (Sexy Stranger) shakes his head, "No, I'm okay. My kids

sometimes forget I'm not a pro wrestler, so it won't be the first or last busted nose."

I laugh, nervously. I can't help but sneak a look at his left finger at the mention of kids, but I see no wedding ring.

Not that it matters. I busted the guy's nose...I highly doubt he's going to stick around and ask for my number afterwards.

While he's pressing the rag to his nose, I drink him in. His hair is dark and tousled, the way I would imagine running his hands through it over and over out of habit would cause it to be. His jaw is sharp, his cheekbones angular, and the lashes framing his bright green eyes are dark and wispy. A stark contrast to the lightness of his eyes.

He's beautiful.

It's rare that you'd call a man beautiful, but this is the only way to describe him. He's the kind of man that you'd look back at twice, just to make sure you weren't dreaming.

Cheesy, but true.

And I'm staring.

My cheeks heat as I tear my eyes from him and focus on the glowing clock above the register.

Ten thirty-four. Less than thirty minutes, and I'm done with this horrible—seemingly getting increasingly worse—night. Hopefully, I make it out unscathed.

"Can I at least get you the house special?" I ask, in an attempt to sway him into at least letting me feed him after I ruined his night. "We have the best burgers in town."

He looks at me for a second, and even with the rag full of blood pressed against his face, he is so handsome it's ridiculous.

No one should look *that* good.

"That would be great. No onions, please."

I nod and walk to the kitchen window, then call out his order to Tommy.

Tommy eyes me warily when he notices the badly bleeding patron in our booth.

"Don't ask." I sigh.

"Wasn't gonna."

I grin and walk back over to SS. The rag is no longer on his nose, and it looks as if the blood has stopped flowing. Thankfully. I'm not sure how much more my stomach can take.

Add that to the utter embarrassment I'm feeling.

"Okay, order is in and you're all set. Can I grab you a drink?"

I shuffle from one foot to the other and fidget nervously with my hands. I'm hoping he doesn't think I'm a total idiot, but chances are...he does.

"Water would be great."

He pulls his phone from his pocket and glances at the screen, then frowns, like he was expecting a notification he doesn't find.

Now that, I understand. I had waited two agonizing days for a response to my job inquiry, and that reminds me...I still haven't responded to the email. I wonder what SS does? Is he a chef? A lawyer? A construction worker? I can see his hands being put to good use.

Using tools, I mean.

Jesus, Juliet, get it together. What am I even thinking about right now? He has me completely frazzled.

I fill his cup with ice, then water, and add lemon and bring it back to his table. Somehow, managing not to spill it all over him. When I approach, he sets his phone down and smiles. A real one, this time, even if it seems reserved.

"Well, I can at least say tonight was interesting," he teases.

"I promise, I only bust people's noses like twice a week. I'm the reigning champ. You know, a UFC waitress. That was lame. Forget I said that."

I almost groan out loud. The man is causing me to spew words that don't even make sense, and I'm pretty sure, if I stay here another second, I'm going to die of embarrassment.

He grins, and the flush hits my cheeks again. This time, it reaches my chest and travels downward. I feel his smile down to my toes.

"I guess next time, I'll have to be more prepared." The green shade of his irises shines with amusement, and I want to reach out and run my thumb along the expanse of his jaw.

Feel the scrape of his scruff across the sensitive pad of my thumb.

"J, order up!" Tommy calls, breaking my trance.

The sound of the plate hitting the counter is enough to tear my gaze from him, and I retrieve his food, then stop to get utensils and napkins before bringing it all back to his booth.

"Here you go. I'm sorry again, sincerely. If you need anything, let me know. "

When he nods, I scurry away before I can embarrass myself any more. I disappear behind the kitchen door, and once it's closed, I press my back against the cold steel, resting my head. I take a deep breath, and then another because one wasn't enough.

"Holy. Shit." I whisper to no one.

Not at all how I saw my night going. I take my second to breathe, then I busy myself doing closing tasks, since we're closing in less than ten minutes. I quickly roll the silverware, then pop back out to the dining room to check on him.

But I walk out and find his table empty. Sexy Stranger no more. When I get to his table, I see a crisp hundred-dollar bill on the table, with a note scrawled on a napkin in messy handwriting.

Next time, I'm putting my money on you, UFC waitress.

I smile so big that my cheeks hurt.

Maybe the day from hell wasn't *so* bad after all?

CHAPTER FIVE
Liam

To Whom It May Concern (You didn't sign your last email, so I'm not sure how to address you):

Simply, to answer your questions:

1. No food allergies, that I'm aware of.
2. Yes, I can braid. Fishtail and French.

When I asked if you had any questions, I expected them in reference to previous employment or my degree.

And in response to the last part of your email, your statement was completely unnecessary. I take my job and my career very seriously, and I have no intention of jeopardizing that in any way...especially for a "date" with you.

I would love the chance to interview for this position, and based upon my resume and your desired qualifications, I think you would be pleased with my performance.

I look forward to speaking with you. Again.

Juliet Michaels

What the hell is a fishtail braid? I've obviously got to watch more YouTube videos because I thought I had the braiding thing down pat.

"Ari, have you ever heard of a fishtail braid?" I ask my daughter. She's perched next to Ken on their giant pink bean bag chair on the floor of the living room as we watch *Frozen* for the millionth time. I lost track about six months ago. But I can recite the lines without subtitles, and that means I've watched it one too many times.

"Oh, yes. Brianne at school always has the most beautiful braids. Her mommy does those braids. She asked me why I only have plain braids, and I told her that you are still learning."

I laugh and shake my head before scanning the email again.

Her sarcasm is apparent...but she's obviously truly interested in the job because she answered the questions I threw in to test her.

Will I be interviewing her and wasting my time on yet another person who isn't what I'm looking for?

I glance at the girls as they begin to sing with Elsa and her talking snowman friend. I needed a nanny, and I have to make a decision. I can't bring them on the road with me and have them sleeping in hotel rooms every night.

After all the interviews I've done, one more won't hurt. If it's a flop, I'll just move on to the next. Although, their resume isn't nearly as impressive as Juliet's.

I type a quick response:

Miss Michaels,

Thank you for answering my questions. Would you be available to come in for an interview tomorrow at 8 AM?

To my surprise, her response comes less than ten minutes later.

To Whom It May Concern (You didn't sign your last email, so I'm not sure how to address you...again):

I'm available at that time and would love to come in for an interview. What's your name? So I can say hello properly when we meet.

Thank you for your consideration.

Juliet Michaels

"Daddy, can we make slime? Please, please?" Ari asks before I can respond.

Oh God. Please, no. Slime will be the death of me. Never, in the history of the world, has there been a toy that makes mess the way this shit does.

It seeps into every nook and cranny, every orifice on every surface of your house. And if you have girls like me, add in confetti and fucking glitter, and you'll never get rid of it.

I'm pretty sure it was created to make parents' lives hell.

Two weeks later, I'll be taking a piss in the bathroom and see a glob of it stuck to the wall, dried and sparkly, taunting me.

"Not tonight bug, slime is messy, and we have an early day tomorrow."

Her bottom lip pokes out in a pout—the same one I give in to way too often—and she puts her hands together, "Please, Daddy. It would make me so very happy."

Christ. Stay strong, Liam. Don't give in to the puppy dog eyes.

"Pwease, Daddy," Ken chimes in, with a similar pouty lip.

"Thirty minutes, and we are not leaving the kitchen table for any reason whatsoever."

They both jump up and down and scream, Elsa forgotten.

I respond to Juliet's email before following them into the kitchen.

Liam.

555 41st St. 8 AM.

I'm up long before the sun the next morning. My internal clock has been set to *early as fuck* since the girls were born and remained that way even after they both slept through the night. It seems like I'm the one who's never able to sleep through the night anymore.

I can't remember the last time I slept past five a.m. Since I'm up way before the girls, I go down to the basement and spend the next hour on the treadmill. I make it a point to stay in the best shape I can, so my morning routine includes three miles on the treadmill, along with another circuit of weights and weighted balls.

Once I'm done, I shower and change into a button down and slacks, then wake the girls up and get their breakfast started.

Just as I pull their toast out of the toaster, Reed walks into the kitchen.

"Uncle Reed!" "ReeRee!", the girls scream as soon as they see him.

Reed is their favorite person, even over my sister, whom they adore. I'd say that it's because he buys them dollhouses that are twice as big as they are, or because he lets them put makeup and an Elsa wig on him, but really, it's because he's shown up. Whenever they were sick, when I needed to breathe—anything, really. Kids crave consistency, and Reed has been a constant since day one. I owe Reed my life, and more. After their mother left, he knew how important it was to me to give them twice the love, twice the affection, and twice the attention. I knew the girls needed people in their lives they could count on, and who would show up, no matter what. I never wanted them to feel like they were missing out on anything because their mother was gone, and Reed had helped me make that a reality.

"My beauties." He drops a kiss on both of their heads before grabbing an apple off the counter.

"Daddy, only green grapes, please!" Ari reminds me.

Like I haven't made her the same breakfast every day for the past three years. She's my bossy one...and the one who likes her schedule to stay the same. Kinda like her dad.

"You got it, bug," I chuckle.

I cut the wheat toast into shapes with the cookie cutter heart before spreading the fruit preserves on them and adding a few "green grapes only" and a few banana slices.

I'm a girl dad, sue me.

And just because I only allow organic, non-GMO, gluten free food in the house, doesn't mean the girls have to sacrifice their heart-shaped food.

"So, ready for your interview today?" Reed asks me casually.

Shrugging, I put away the bread and jar before turning back to him, eyeing him warily, "Just another interview. Hopefully, it works out so I can stop stressing the..." I look towards the girls and whisper under my breath, hidden by my hand, "fuck out."

"I'm sure it'll be great. Last night, when you called, I googled her." He shrugs.

"Really? You're as invasive as my damn mother."

His laugh echoes through the kitchen, as if it's the funniest thing he's ever heard. Dick.

"Nah, your mother would've reached out and set you two up by now."

Damnit. He's right. My mother is famous for setting me up with any and every female she deems respectable.

Before I can respond, the doorbell rings, and a grin tugs at the corner of his lips. "Show time."

"Please, for the love of God, keep the girls *out* of the slime. And no markers. Especially those of permanent variety."

He tries to argue, but I stop him, "No, dude. I'm still using that damn magic eraser to scrub it off the wall. I'll be back as soon as I'm finished."

He volunteered to watch the girls during the interview, and I'm not sure the house will still be standing, but I don't have time to find anyone else, so here we are.

"No slime." I say, pointing my finger at him, "I'm serious."

I quickly drop a kiss on the girls' heads then check my watch as I walk to the front door.

Seven fifty-nine. Early, with a minute to spare. At least we're going to start off on the right foot.

I swing the door open and am completely thrown off guard when, standing on the other side, is the same girl from the other night.

Diner Girl.

She seems just as surprised as me because her jaw is slack, and her eyes widen. The waitress uniform is gone, and instead, she's wearing a black, fitted dress that accentuates her waist, and I'm sure if she turns around, her ass.

For fuck's sake. We haven't even properly introduced ourselves, and I'm already thinking of her ass. My eyes flit back to her face, and I realize I've been caught. Her manicured eyebrows are raised high. Today, she's wearing her hair down in wavy curls that fall past her shoulders. Much longer than I would've expected, and it only makes her more beautiful, if that's even possible.

Clearly, it is. Her long, dark hair, paired with the burnt gold honey of her eyes, has me stifling a groan at the sight of her.

She's dangerous.

"God, it looks even worse today," she says. And by "it", she means my nose. After she accidentally almost broke it two days ago.

"Thanks."

Her cheeks pink, "I—I...I'm sorry, that was rude. I just mean that the bruising is rather bad."

I nod, "So, you're Juliet."

"And you're Liam."

"And you're here to interview for the nanny position." I pause, and she nods, "So, come in." I hold the door open so she can pass in front of me, but she doesn't make a move to come inside.

"Wait, you're still going to give me a chance?"

She looks genuinely confused.

"Why wouldn't I?"

"Well...I mean, I almost broke your nose."

I almost laugh, but I shake my head and shrug, "It was an accident, Juliet. Come inside, and we can get to the interview. Unless, it's you who's changed your mind?"

"No, no." Her words come out in a rush. She smiles and brushes past me into the foyer. I can't help when my eyes drop to her ass as she walks further into the house. I was right, her dress hugs her... everywhere.

This is completely inappropriate, but I can't help the stolen glance.

I avert my eyes right before she turns around and smiles, "Your home is beautiful."

"Thank you. Right this way," I lead her into my office, and once she's seated in front of my desk in the plush chair, I shut the door behind us.

Hopefully, Reed will be able to wrangle the girls long enough that I'm able to actually interview Diner Girl. I mean, Juliet.

What are the odds that she'd be the same girl from the other night? The same one that I couldn't stop thinking about, even long after I'd left the diner. Even when I'd spent the rest of the night propped up in bed, icing my nose. I'm a retired hockey player. I've beat the shit out of people and had the shit beaten out of me, yet this girl somehow still managed to give me the bloody nose of a lifetime.

I pull her resume out from the folder and set it in front of me, then look at her. She seems nervous, but also confident. The black dress on her chest dips when she leans forward slightly, and I'm doing everything in my fucking power to look anywhere but there.

Juliet is breathtaking. It's not that I hadn't noticed the other night. I did, even with a bloody nose. She's fucking gorgeous. Dark hair, eyes that are gold, almost like warm honey that melts against your tongue. She seems like the type of woman who doesn't even realize the power behind her beauty.

"So, I guess we just jump right in it. Tell me about yourself." I say, leaning back in my desk chair.

"Well, I'm twenty-two. I'm a senior in college, working on my early childhood education degree."

I stop her before she can continue, "Tell me about what I can't read on the resume. Why do you want this job?"

What I'm asking for wasn't what was typed on this piece of paper. I want beyond that. I've read her resume enough over the last few days that I can recite it with my eyes closed. Her academic accomplishments and the details of her college education, what her high school was, what skills she excelled at. I don't want to hear that.

I want to know why she wants this job. What is she like when the door is closed and the world is shut out?

She's quiet, looking down at her hands in her lap before looking back up at me. Her honey eyes, liquid and molten, pour into mine.

"My Nana. She's in a nursing home downtown. A few months ago, while I was working a shift at the diner, she fell and broke her hip in three places. She had to have a total hip replacement...and at her age, despite how healthy she is, the doctor is worried. That's why I'd like to take this job. So I can afford to keep her there. She's my best friend, and I would be lost without her."

"Why are you working at a diner, when you could be finishing school and graduating?" I ask, genuinely curious.

"Every job that I've applied for needs someone with a degree. And right now, I have to take care of my Nana. I can't go back to school until we're in a better financial situation."

I'm shocked by her honesty. Not many people would be so forthcoming.

"I appreciate your honesty. The truth is, you're more than qualified for this position, even without a degree in hand. This position is a live-in position, and I will be gone for six months out of the year."

Her eyes widen in surprise.

"So...like—you...won't be here at all with the children?"

I shake my head, "I've just recently taken a position with the Avalanche as their new head coach. The season is grueling. We spend six months on the road, when it's all said and done. The person I'm looking for needs to be committed and dedicated. I have two girls, and they'll require all of your attention. It's why the salary is so generous. I don't want anyone who's going to take the position and then decide a month later that they can't handle it. The most important things to me for my girls are consistency and structure."

She nods and pulls her plump, glossy lip between her teeth, "I'm still interested in the job. I don't have a social life like most women my age. The only thing I would want is to visit my Nana on the weekends, unless you're away at a game, of course. I could plan around another day to visit her."

"Whenever I'm home, your time is yours. Whenever I'm not, that's the time that you would be on duty, however long that may be. I have my schedule for the next year, but sometimes, things change. I'm looking for someone for the long term."

Before she can speak, a piercing scream followed by "Dadddddddddddddy!!!" rings out through my office.

Ari's scream pierces through the door, sending me out of my chair so fast it topples backwards. I'm out the door and running down the stairs and towards the living room in a matter of seconds. Juliet must have followed behind me because I catch a glimpse of her brunette hair when I turn the corner into the living room.

I find Ari and Ken on top of the coffee table clutching each other, and no Reed in sight.

What the hell?

"Ari, bug, what's wrong?"

"Daddy…a mouse, a real one, under the bucket!" she cries and points towards the floor.

Oh, for fuck's sake.

"Where is Uncle Reed?"

Kennedy points to the door leading to the back patio. I can see that Reed is outside on the phone.

"He had to take an intorta-nt phone call and then the mouse ran across the floor! I trapped it. In my bucket."

Tears wet her cheeks as she sobs, and if this isn't the most dramatic thing I've ever seen in my life, then I don't know what it is.

"It's okay baby, Daddy will take care of it, okay? Dry your tears." I murmur. I pick them both up off the table and set them on the floor...far from the mouse in question.

Neither of them looks like they feel any better about the situation, so I'd better get rid of the damn thing before there's another meltdown and I never get to finish the interview. I walk to the kitchen to grab something to help me keep the mouse inside the bucket and finally find something.

When I return to the living room, the girls don't even notice me walk up. Juliet is squatting down in front of them, wiping stray tears from their cheeks.

"I know how scary that must have been for you. But your Daddy is strong and brave, and he will take care of it for you, okay?" she says softly.

Ari looks at her and smiles, revealing her two dimples, "My Daddy is the best. He always watches *Frozen* with us, and he always braids my hair! What's your name?"

"My name is Juliet."

"Why you here?" Kennedy asks her.

Juliet smiles and lowers her voice to a whisper, using her hand to shield her mouth. From my position at the door, I can still hear what she's saying, "Wanna know a secret?"

They both nod profusely. Ari whispers yells, "Yes! I *love* secrets."

"Well, this is a very important one, and you have to pinky promise to never tell."

Ari looks at Kennedy with wide eyes, then back at Juliet.

"We pwomise," Kennedy whispers. Or well…it's not really so much of a whisper.

I bite back a laugh when she raises her small pinky for Juliet.

Pinky promises are the ultimate promise in this house. Not that Juliet knows that.

"Okay…are you ready? I think your daddy *might* be a….knight in shining armor."

They gasp as if they understand the term. Both of their faces are filled with awe, and fuck if I don't feel a pang somewhere deep in my gut. Something I haven't felt in a very long time.

"And do you know what that makes you? Princesses."

The girls jump up and down squealing before she says, "Shhh."

"But, are you a princess, Juli? Your hair is pretty like a princess'."

Juliet's smile widens, and she twirls a piece of Ari's hair around her finger, "I wish that I was a princess, but you girls will have to tell me what it's like."

Not that I couldn't watch my girls with a genuine smile on their faces all day, but Ari has to get to school, and this interview is officially over. I've seen everything I need to see. Combined with her resume, it's the only logical choice. I step forward and clear my throat.

All three of them look at me, then at each other, and Ari and Ken collapse in a fit of giggles. The mouse has been completely forgotten. And then I realize that was Juliet's plan all along. Make them comfortable and distract them with knights in shining armor

and princesses.
And that makes me realize the most important thing of all.
Juliet is going to be the nanny. I don't even need to really think about it. It was done the second I saw her interact with them. Never mind the fact that I can't stop stealing glances at her when she's not looking. She's so off limits, it hasn't even crossed my mind.
At all.
Not even in that tight, black dress that shows off every—
You know what? No. Not thinking of it at all.
I've finally found someone who's at least qualified to care for the girls, and even though she's clumsy and rather timid, she's the best candidate so far.
The last thing I would ever do is put my job in jeopardy by thinking about the new nanny with the princess hair and honey eyes.

CHAPTER SIX
Juliet

"Nana, you do realize how outrageous that sounds, right?" I ask. She's sitting across from me, knitting something with neon orange yarn, and I'm kind of scared to ask what, for fear that she'll say it's for me.

There's a scoff, followed by, "Well Juliet, I'm just saying. You're twenty-two years old, and now you're working for a retired hockey player. You need a man. A hot one who has lots of money and a nice butt. Have you seen their butts?"

"Can we *not* talk about my new boss' butt? Like, can this not be a thing?" I groan and drop my head onto my arms on the table.

Leave it to Nana to try her hand at matchmaking me with the one person who is the absolute last man I should ever try and date. Ever.

Like ever ever.

Not only has he made it abundantly clear that he will not be having any sort of relationship with his nanny, which should be a given—I think—but I also don't think he finds me attractive, whatsoever. He seems pretty uncomfortable any time I'm in his vicinity.

Imagine my surprise when he'd opened the door, and I'd realized he was *Sexy Stranger* from the diner. I'd almost swallowed my tongue. I'd only had a moment to recover because he'd been as surprised as me.

"Don't be a prude, Juliet."

My eighty-four-year-old grandmother is calling me a prude. That says a lot.

"Just because I am not interested in hitting on my boss does not mean I'm a prude, Nana! My God," I huff.

Her eyebrows raise, "When was the last time you went on a date? A real one."

I bite my lip while I think. It has actually been a while, but I think the last time was with a guy that Alex hooked me up with. And, well, that had been such a disaster I really don't think I'll ever date again.

A shiver racks my body at the memory. The guy had smelled so strongly of body odor that I accidentally gagged a bit during dinner, then I'd faked an emergency on the phone with Nana. It had been traumatizing.

"That was the BO guy. And the time before that was the guy who was very attached to his mother. In like...a weird way."

She rolls her eyes dramatically, then looks at her best friend, "Gladys, tell her about the fella you used to date."

Gladys Andrews is Nana's best friend, and one third of the Golden Girls, as I like to call them. Gladys was a show girl in

Vegas in her former life, and she doesn't let a day go by without reminding us of it. When I say the woman has more stories and wisdom than you can possibly imagine, I'm not exaggerating.

Some of her stories were so enthralling they kept me here for hours, hanging on every last word. By the end, she'd have painted such a vivid picture that it played like a movie in my head. Gladys could tell a story like no other.

So, it's no surprise that Nana has looked to Gladys to pipe in about my non-existent love life.

Gladys looks at me over the top of her glasses, which are an exact replica from the eighties, bright pink color and all, "Oh Betty, are you referring to the one that was hung like the Italian stallion?" She sighs dreamily.

Jesus, these three will be the death of me.

Nana giggles, "Yes! Isn't the saying one you go Italian, you never go back? Or something of the sort. Go on, tell her."

"I'm pretty sure that is not actually the saying," I quip, and Gladys shakes her head of light pink hair.

"That man was a dream. You know, I still think about him sometimes, even all these years later. A man like that sure does leave a lasting impression..."

They both giggle like they're still teenagers, and it's impossible not to smile alongside them.

"You two are impossible. Where is Judith today?" I ask, noticing that she hasn't joined us this morning.

"Oh, she should be here soon. She was tidying her room this morning."

My phone vibrates on the table, causing it to echo throughout the room. When I open it, I see an email from Liam, and my heart speeds up.

I've been trying not to get my hopes up, but it was hard not to. I need this job badly, and even more than that...I want it. Liam's little girls are the cutest, and I feel like we connected while I was there.

My fingers shake as I open the email and begin reading

Juliet,

I want to thank you for interviewing with me yesterday. I know that it wasn't a typical interview, but judging by the way you interacted with the girls, and your resume, you seem to have the qualifications needed. I won't waste any time in saying this. I'd like to you offer you the position.

I pause reading to clutch my chest because, holy shit, I wasn't expecting to actually get it, let alone for him to offer it less than twenty-four hours after the interview.

If you accept the offer, I would like you to start immediately. Of course, there is a lot for us to review and discuss, and I am on a tight schedule, but I will be able to do that as early as tomorrow morning.

Please let me know what you think and if you will be accepting the position. If so, please respond, and we can discuss the logistics of your new residency here.

Liam

Wow. I actually got the job. I'm going to be a live-in nanny, taking care of the sweetest little girls...full time.

"What's wrong, Juliet?" Nana asks. I look up and see her soft eyes filled with concern. "You look like you've seen a ghost, darling."

"No, no." I start, "I just...got the job."

Gladys squeals and puts her hand up for Nana to high five. "I told you that you would, Juliet! He will be lucky to have you."

"Thank you, Nana. Now, I have to pack up all my things to basically move into his house. It feels, I don't know, different than I expected."

I feel guilty for saying that, and it's mostly the nervousness talking, but it is weird to move into a stranger's house. I need this job, truly. I don't have time for nervousness to take root. Not taking this job isn't an option.

"Let your Nana tell you a secret, darling. Come here," She pats the seat next to her on the floral loveseat. The knitting she's been working on is put aside, and she turns to face me as I sit down next to her.

"You are smart, kind, and beautiful from the outside in. Every part of you."

The tears well behind my eyes before I have the chance to stop them. When my parents passed away in a tragic car accident when I was only seven, Nana had taken me in. She had done her dues, raised my mother, and was getting ready to travel the world. Then, suddenly, I was thrown into her lap. She never once faltered and never made me feel like a burden. She'd loved me and raised me to be the best woman I could be. I would not be who I am today without her love and guidance.

"Oh, Nana," I cry.

"Shh, darling, no tears. You will excel at this job, just like you do every other aspect of your life. Don't be nervous. Walk in with your head held high, and show him just how amazing you are. Remember, life is what you make it."

"And snatch him up the second you get a chance," Gladys chimes in.

I laugh, then shake my head and swipe away the tears from my cheeks.

Nana grabs my hand and holds it in her soft, wrinkled hand. Her grip is strong and resilient, and I hope that she will be here for a lot longer for me to love, and to give me her advice and wisdom.

"You're right. Change is just hard. I'm thankful, and I'm excited. You have to meet his little girls, Ari and Kennedy. They are the most precious angels."

Nana's eyes light up, "I would love too, darling."

Our moment is interrupted when Judith walks up and sits next to Gladys. Her hair is brushed and slicked back, as always. Come to think of it, I've never actually seen her wear her light grey hair down. It's always pulled back tightly off the nape of her neck. Today, she's wearing a dark green sweat suit and black Converse.

"What are you two boohooing about?"

Oh, Judith. She's the tough one of the trio. It's rare that you see her soft side come out. Tough as nails and solid as a concrete wall. Nothing gets past her.

"Juliet is taking a new job for a famous hockey coach. As his nanny! Isn't it so exciting?" Gladys exclaims.

Judith's eyebrows raise, "Oh, now this *is* exciting news. Is he rich?"

"Judith!"

She shrugs, "Take it from me, men are only good for one thing, and it's not what's in their pants. Get you a man with money, and all your problems are solved."

Gladys guffaws, "You are bitter, you old hag. Juliet isn't a gold digger. She's looking for love."

"Yeah, what she said," Nana quips, picking up her knitting and continuing the bright orange monstrosity, "You're just mad that a certain miser isn't interested in you, but maybe if you were a little less ice cold with him.'

That causes me to whip my head to Nana, "Wait, Judith has a crush? Who is it?"

Judith doesn't let her answer, "Don't go spreadin' my business around, Betty. I don't want that old fart. He shares his jello. It doesn't mean there's a romantic connection going on.

"We all know it Judith, but the sooner you admit it to yourself the better," Nana says.

"Mhm, that's right," Gladys says.

These three are a hoot. I'm feeling much better after talking to Nana and taking a few deep breaths.

I'm ready to start a new chapter in my life.

I pull my phone out and reply to Liam's email.

Liam,

I accept. Shall I be there at 8t AM?

I have a feeling this new chapter will be the best of them all.

CHAPTER SEVEN
Liam

"Is she here yet?" Ari asks.

For the tenth time. In the past five minutes.

When I explained to the girls that Juliet is going to be their new nanny, I honestly wasn't expecting as much excitement as I got. Ari squealed so loudly I was sure my eardrum had burst, and Kennedy cried and told me she was so thankful.

As much as I didn't want Juliet to work out, because of my own aversions, she seems to be the perfect nanny for the girls.

"Not yet, bug. Hey, how about we do some coloring until she gets here? Waiting at the window won't make time move any faster. But I bet Juliet would love it if you colored her a picture. Ken? What do you say?"

Begrudgingly, Ari drops down from the chair she's standing in to look out the window, walks over to the kitchen table, and plops down.

"It feels like time is moving extra slow today, Daddy."

I laugh, "Well, that's because you're excited, bug, and you're waiting by the window. Your grandma used to tell me that watched pots never boil. Same thing here. Waiting by the window won't make her get here any quicker. Plus… it's only breakfast time, so not that long."

She sticks out her lip in a pout.

Then Ken follows suit.

Monkey see, monkey do. It's not surprising that everything Ari does, Ken isn't far behind her.

I busy myself trying to organize the binder I put together late last night for Juliet. After I got her email that she would be accepting the position, I started to put together everything I could think of that would help her transition into the nanny position.

And, although she is going to be the new nanny, I want to keep any and all communication between us to a bare minimum. The last thing I need is to find myself alone with Juliet and tempted even more by her plump lips and honey-colored eyes.

This was going to be a fucking disaster if that happened. Therefore, I'm going to prevent it.

The binder has all pertinent information. Dates of birth, allergies, doctors, my parents' and Shana's numbers, insurance information. The number to the front office, Reed's cell, foods they like and dislike, and foods—like sugar and candy—that they are not allowed to have.

I keep our meals meticulously planned, balancing all food groups, and only on one occasion a year do my girls get candy. Call me what you want, but their health comes first, and I'm not going to bog down their bodies with all of that processed junk.

"Daddy?" Ken asks.

"Hmm?"

"The doorbell, Daddy! She's here! She's here!" Ari yells and dashes from her seat before I can stop her. She comes to a screeching stop at the door and wrenches it open.

"Ari Rose!" I exclaim, running behind her with Kennedy trailing behind me. She looks up at me with a wide grin, then back at Juliet, who's standing on the other side of the door.

"Hi," she says, almost shyly.

"Hi, sorry about that. Ari knows she's not supposed to answer the door, but she's excited to have you here. Come in."

I pick Ari up and move her out the way as Juliet walks in, rolling a lavender colored suitcase behind her. It makes this so much more real seeing her with the suitcase. For a second, I doubt myself. Then, Kennedy launches herself at Juliet and wraps her tiny arms around Juliet's legs, holding on for dear life.

"Ken, give her some space, baby."

Juliet smiles, then shakes her head, "No, it's okay. Hi, Princess Kennedy."

Kennedy looks up at her, giggling.

"Can we play now, Juliet? I got all my Barbies out and my babies, and my slime..."

"Uh, bug, me and Miss Juliet have a lot of things to discuss. You're going to have reading time while we go over it, okay?"

Ari and Kennedy both look crestfallen, but Juliet bends down and takes each of their hands before speaking in a soft voice, "Me and your daddy just have some castle business to attend to, but I promise, as soon as we are done and I am settled in my new room, I will come and we can play Barbies for the rest of the day."

"Pinky promise?" Ari asks, holding out her pinky.

"Pinky promise."

Their pinkies intertwine, sealing the deal, and the girls scamper off towards the living room, each picking their favorite book from the shelf before settling on the couch to read quietly.

Wow. That might be the easiest the girls have ever done *anything*.

"Sorry about that. I told them last night that you were going to be their new nanny, and they have been bursting at the seams with excitement ever since."

She laughs, a soft, sensual sound that tumbles from her lips easily. One that immediately shoots to my dick, and I clear my throat before I end up embarrassing the both of us.

What the fuck is wrong with you, Liam? I never have this type of reaction to a woman so quickly.

"So, I'll go ahead and show you to your room so you can put your things away, and then we can discuss everything."

I decided last night that I wouldn't do anything to encourage my attraction to Juliet, and if that means that we aren't going to be able to be friendly, then so be it.

Together, we walk down the hallway to the other side of the house, where both girls' rooms are, as well as the master. I point out each room to her, and let her know that her room will be on the second floor, next to my office and the other guest room. I quickly take her to the basement and show her the home gym.

"You're welcome to use the gym at any time. The passcode down here is eight-three-seven-four. I keep it locked at all times because of the equipment. The girls get...enthusiastic about things, and I don't want them to get hurt. Please keep this locked. "

"Okay, no problem. I understand."

Her eyes catch mine, and for a brief moment I think that I see something simmering behind them. Something I hadn't seen before, and something that resonates inside of me. The same feeling that I've felt since she walked back through the door. Lust.

Fuck, the walls of the hallway seem to shrink in with us pressed against them. I've never realized, until this moment, how tight of a space it is.

I can smell the sweet, clean scent of her perfume, and even though it's wrong, and forbidden, I want to lean closer and run my nose along the delicate skin of her throat.

Fuck, what am I thinking? This cannot happen. I need to nip this shit in the bud. Now.

Suddenly, the air feels even thicker as something moves between us. Something I have no control over, which leaves me feeling out of control. Reckless.

And, just as quickly as it started, I damper it back down, "Okay," I clear my throat, "You can freshen up while I get the girls ready to draw. It'll keep them occupied for a while."

"Yes. Of course. Thank you." She says, breathily.

I brush past her towards the living room, wondering what in the absolute hell I've gotten myself into, and how I stop it.

The entire day passed so quickly, I lost track of time as I showed Juliet around the house and gave her the rundown of everything.

"That's it. Everything you need will be in here. This is my number—be sure to program it into your phone. I'll call nightly or FaceTime to talk to the girls before bed. If you have any questions, you can give me a call. Or text, if I'm at the rink. Emergency contacts are at the back here," I say, flipping to the page that has a list of all of the emergency contacts, including my sister.

"Wow. This is...comprehensive." Her eyes are wide, and she seems a bit overwhelmed, but I created this so she'll have a go-to if there is anything she doesn't know.

"Daddy is anal." Ari quips. She's coloring yet another Elsa picture, to go alongside the other three she's completed in the last hour. Each of them is pink and purple and match the play princess dress she's wearing with a matching tiara. Kennedy is wearing a Cinderella dress up gown with matching heels and tiara, complete with necklace and bracelets.

Juliet laughs out loud at her admission.

"Wow, that's quite a vocabulary, Ari."

She shrugs, "My Auntie Shana calls Daddy that."

Sometimes it blows my mind that I've raised these two beautiful girls all on my own. Hell, I was barely more than a kid myself when I had them. Sure, I was in my late twenties, but I was still maturing. Growing. I'd cared more about money, partying, and living it up than I had anything else.

Then, Ari came along and changed my life. I'd wanted to be better for her. I'd wanted to be the type of father that people raved about, not the one who ended up in tabloids for another scandal. I left all that shit behind. I traded the booze for sippy cups, puck bunnies for princess dress up, and the partying for nights on the couch with both of them snuggled against my side. I wouldn't trade it for the damn world. They are everything to me.

"What did we say about repeating things Aunt Shana says?" I ask sternly.

She looks down, "I'm not 'posed to because Auntie Shana says things that my ears shouldn't hear."

THE NEWSPAPER NANNY

"Right. Go ahead and go play in your room with Ken while Miss Juliet and I talk, okay? She can come see your Barbies after dinner."

Ari nods energetically.

"You're amazing with them, Liam." Juliet says once Ari's out of ear shot.

I shrug, "It's my job. They're my girls, and I'd do anything for them."

Juliet sits down at the bar and laces her hands together in front of her. I notice the chipped, pale pink polish on the nails of her dainty, thin fingers. I can't help but notice things about her. Things I shouldn't notice.

"So, you're leaving in a few days for an away game?"

I start making dinner while we're talking, desperate for something to do with my hands to distract me, "Yeah. I'll be in New York for a night, then fly home the next day. I have to fly with the team."

"Did you like being a player...before coaching?" she asks. There is genuine curiosity in her eyes, but I see she must have googled me. I guess I would've done the same thing before I moved into a strange guy's house.

I sigh, "Hockey was my life. You know, before the girls. I lived it, I breathed it. Everything I did was for my career. I grew with a pair of skates and a stick. It was kind of a given that I'd end up in the pros." I clear my throat, ready to steer the subject away from me.

"I don't mean to pry...or be nosy, I just... is their mother still around at all? You haven't mentioned her."

The question causes ice to flood my veins. The girls' mother is the one topic I'll never be discussing, and as of now, this conversation is finished.

"We don't discuss her, so please do not bring her up around the girls," I say, my voice cold and blunt.

"I'm sorry, I—" she starts, but stops, realizing I'm done talking.

It was a mistake, even telling her this much about my life. I'm already letting my attraction to her cloud my judgement. I don't know what the fuck I was thinking. The one thing that I can't, and won't do.

Juliet is the nanny, nothing more.

My personal life, and the life I had before my girls, has nothing do with her.

"I'm going to check on the girls," I say, leaving her sitting at the bar alone. Hot and cold, but it doesn't matter. I'm not discussing Carrie. Now, or ever.

Hours later, I still feel frustration stirring in my chest. Juliet and I had only discussed the coming days and nothing more. She seemed to understand that I wanted distance and space from her after her questions.

I almost feel bad, but I have to protect my girls first and foremost, and talking about the person who abandoned them isn't what they need. I failed at protecting them once before, and it will never happen again.

"Juliet, do you have a mommy?" Ari asks. Juliet is brushing Ari's hair after bath time, and Ari is wrapped in her furry pink robe. I let

THE NEWSPAPER NANNY

Juliet handle bath time tonight to see the girls' routine, and I only observed and made a comment when needed.

It's apparent that she's going to be great with the girls.

It doesn't stop my heart from seizing in my chest at her question.

Juliet looks at her and smiles sadly, "No, Ari, I don't. She's in Heaven. When I was a little girl, not much older than you, she went to be in Heaven. I miss her very much."

Ari looks at the sash around her waist and fidgets with it before looking back up at Juliet, "My mommy is gone, too. I'm not sure where she is, but I don't think she's in Heaven."

Fuck, she looks so sad it breaks my heart. She never brings Carrie up with me, ever. I didn't know she even really realized that she has a different home life than other kids. Guilt claws its way up my chest, seizing me wholly. I work so hard to protect them from the things that can hurt them, but she has been thinking this without me even realizing.

"Well, Ari, I know that it might make you sad, sometimes. And it's okay to be sad. But, you have so many people who love you. They love you enough to make up for anyone who's not here to love you. Your daddy, Uncle Reed, Aunt Shana. Even me."

"You love me?"

My kind-hearted, sensitive girl.

"Of course, I do." Juliet keeps running the brush through Ari's long blonde hair, and I realize that I haven't heard one complaint from Ari at all. Holy shit, did she get through an entire brush without tears? Juliet drops down to her knees in front of Ari and sets the brush to the side before speaking, "You are a princess, Ari, don't forget it. The entire kingdom will protect and love you, no matter what. You and Kennedy are very special."

"Well, since I'm a princess, doesn't that mean I can stay up and watch Sophia the First? She's a princess too, you know."

Juliet throws her head back, and that sweet laughter fills the room. Ari joins her, giggling into her hand.

"You, sweet girl, are right. You're both princesses, and trust me, princesses need all of the beauty sleep they can get. Now, go on and get into bed, and I'm sure Daddy will be in soon. I have to go see Ken and make sure her hair is brushed, too."

Ari nods and bites her bottom lip in thought. The next thing I know, she throws her arms around Juliet's neck and whispers, "Thank you for taking care of us, Juliet. Daddy needed some help, even though he's a knight."

Juliet looks up and her eyes connect with mine as she nods, "I know Ari, sometimes we all do."

CHAPTER EIGHT
Juliet

"This is so much fun, Juliet!" Ari cries as she jumps up and down on the couch. Each time she jumps, her hair bounces with her. It's a mass of blonde and curls that I'm learning have to be tamed with detangler and serum.

This was not what I had in mind when I suggested a sleepover with all three of us in the living room. Both of them are still trying to adjust to Liam being gone, so I suggested we have a sleepover and watch their favorite movie with some popcorn.

Our first night had gone off without a hitch, but the second is proving to be more difficult. You'd think I slipped something extremely sugary into their drinks tonight.

"Alright, Princess Ari, it's time to settle down, so we can watch a movie and eat our popcorn."

Kennedy giggles from the couch, her blonde ringlets falling in her eyes, "Yeah Ari, pwease!"

Neither of them follow my directions, and I'm two seconds from having to raise my voice when my phone rings, and I look down to see Liam's name across the screen.

Tiny, traitorous butterflies erupt in my stomach at the sight of his name, and I tell myself not to be a fool. Regardless of what I tell myself, they seem to come every time I think of him or see his name on my phone.

Which is completely foolish and naive, and I know it.

After the way he'd shut down during our last conversation, I hadn't tried to pursue another conversation. Obviously, it's a sore subject, and now he's closed off and cold when it comes to me.

"Girls, girls, shhh, shhh, time to quiet down. Your daddy is calling."

They squeal and both scramble towards me as I slide the bar to answer his call.

"Hi," I say the moment that he comes into view.

His smile is bright, and it widens when he sees the girls. No one should be this handsome. And I should not be feeling this way. But I can't help it. That's what makes this so much worse. I'm his new nanny, and the last thing that would be good for either of us is to have some...attraction to each other. One we can never act on.

His hair is wet and pushed back off his forehead, obviously freshly showered. He's wearing a simple grey tee and what looks like sweatpants.

Ugh. Nana was right, he does have a great butt. Guys with great butts aren't talked about enough.

"Juliet?" he asks, confusion marring his brow.

I clear my throat, "Uh, sorry, I zoned out."

"How are the girls?"

Ari grins from beside me and pulls on my arm, so I turn the phone toward her and Ken again.

"Hi Daddy!" "Daddy!" they scream. So loudly my ears ring.

I laugh and hand the phone to Ari. She puts it so close to her face, the only thing you can see on the screen is her forehead, and Liam laughs.

"Bug, you have to pull the phone back so I can see both of your pretty faces."

Ari is struggling, with her little arms, to hold it out far enough without dropping it or pointing it towards the ceiling. They're both so excited they can't sit still, and they're talking over each other.

"Daddy, I have on my Elsa nightgown, see? See?"

"Daddy, I miss yew. Can yeeeew come home?"

"Oh, guess what! I learned today that kangaroos have a pouch."

"Daddy, Daddy, Dadddyyyyyy"

I can't help but laugh as I take the phone back from the girls, "Sorry, they're a bit excited."

"It's not a problem. I miss them, too. How is everything?"

I glance around the living room, which looks like a tornado of Barbies, babies, and *Frozen* dolls hit it. There is something on every surface.

"Uh, you know, it is great. It'll be an adjustment, but we will be fine."

He nods, his gaze holding mine for a minute. Then he says, "Well, I've got to get off. We have a long day of traveling tomorrow. I should be home by tomorrow night. Thanks, Juliet."

The girls tell him goodbye and give him their "I love you's" before he hangs up.

"Juliet?" Ari asks. Finally, she's calmed down and is snuggled up against my side as we all three sink into the couch.

"Yes?" I lean forward to take a sip of my water, suddenly parched from the conversation.

"Do you think you could marry my daddy?"

I choke on the water mid-sip, and some of it sprays from my mouth as I sputter and cough, trying to catch my breath.

My God.

"Ari, that's...I—I'm...uh...," I stutter.

Her blue eyes search mine, and then she pulls her bottom lip between her teeth, "Well, you know, we could use a mommy, and my friend Brianna says that mommies and daddies have to be married if they live in the same house."

I'm so shocked for a moment, I don't immediately respond. What are they teaching these kids at school?

"Well, I'm your nanny, Ari. I take care of you when your daddy isn't here, and then, when he comes home, I'll only help out when he needs me. We work together, like a team. Kind of like how your daddy is the coach of his team? He's the coach here at home, too, and I'm just part of the team."

Great, I basically just explained my non-existent love life to a five-year-old.

Ken looks at me and furrows her brows, "Mawwy?"

I bite back the laugh that bubbles up, "You'll understand one day, sweet girl."

"I'm glad you came to take care of us, Juliet. You're the best." Ari squeezes me tight.

And I feel my heart squeeze tight in the process. It's only been a few days, but I find myself falling hard for these girls. They're impossible not to love. And as I turn Elsa on and cover the three of us with a blanket, I feel like I might have found a place for myself, doing something I love.

When Ari falls asleep, tucked tightly against me, while playing with a lock of my hair, and Kennedy's small hand is still laced within mine, I think that there is no other place that I am meant to be.

The next day, Liam is set to return home, and I've decided I'm going to welcome him home with dinner...except everything in his freezer and pantry is giving me hives.

Who *actually* eats this crap?

I pick up the first package I reach for and immediately shudder when I read the front.

Gluten free...grass-fed meatballs?

Gross.

I put the package back and pick up another, which seems to be a package of chicken breasts.

No artificial growth hormones or antibiotics added. Organic...cage free?

Wait, cage free chickens? Okay, next.

I dig further into the freezer and find an unopened bag of chicken nuggets at the bottom. Yes! Finally, something I can cook that isn't weird and...healthy. I shudder.

Gluten free, non-GMO, organic chicken nuggets.

Seriously? Is this guy for real? He's torturing these poor kids. I'm pretty sure these chicken nuggets are going to taste like unseasoned cardboard.

Back in the freezer they go.

Finally, I grab the hamburger meat and decide on meatloaf. Everyone loves meatloaf. Even if it's grass-fed and organic and all of the health nut stuff that Liam requires. I don't need to check the three-inch-thick binder to know that vegetables are non-negotiable, so I grab green beans and some broccoli to roast.

Wow.

"What is it, Juliet?" Ari asks me, clutching her Princess Sparkles unicorn. The pale pink unicorn has obviously seen better days. Its fur is now a suspicious brown color, and it's missing a plastic eyeball. I make a mental note to scour Amazon for another.

You know, for someone who's this worried about organic, non-GMO chicken nuggets...the guy is obviously not worried about germs. This thing probably has the bubonic plague.

"Hmm?"

"You said wow."

Shit, I didn't even realize I had said it out loud.

"Uh...just looking at things for dinner. Does your daddy always make you eat vegetables and healthy things?"

She nods, "Always." Her face is so serious I almost laugh. I saw what he put in the binder, but I guess I hadn't realized how strict he truly is about it.

"No sugar?"

"Never." She shakes her head.

"Wow."

I send her back to the living room to play and finish putting together the mostly healthy dinner, but throw together a quick batch of Nana's famous rolls and hope that he doesn't have heart

THE NEWSPAPER NANNY

failure over gluten-filled carbs.

When he walks through the door, our gaze meets over the bar for a brief second before the girls just about tackle him to the floor with hugs. He laughs and wraps his arms around them tight.

"Hi, my beautiful girls. Wow, you must have *really* missed me."

Ari nods her head enthusiastically, "Oh we did, Daddy! Soooo much. But, we had so much fun with, Juliet. Tonight, we have to watch the new movie she showed us!"

He looks over at me with his eyebrows raised, "New movie, huh? Which one is that?"

"*Moana!*" they scream.

I see the dread and horror on his face, but he quickly corrects it before plastering on a tight smile, "Oh joy. More princesses. Ca*nnot* possibly wait."

"She's the princess of the water, Daddy. I've decided that I will be a water princess, too. I'm going to practice tonight in the bathtub!"

"You do that, bug. How about dinner, and then we can watch it after your baths? How does that sound? Ken?" He looks at Kennedy, and she grins, attacking his leg once more.

He nods in my direction but stays across the bar.

"Hi," I say.

"Hi, everything looks great. Thank you for cooking. Smells great."

I shrug, "It's not a problem. The girls were playing quietly, and I figured you could use something to come home to. I mean, to eat."

A flush creeps up my neck as the corner of his mouth turns up in a small smile. The only one I've seen since our strained conversation days ago.

It's hard to believe I've been here almost a week already. Since Liam is home today and tomorrow, I'm going to Everwood Manor to visit Nana and fill her in about how the past week has gone.

Ari has already begged and pleaded for me to bring her with me, but since I haven't spoken to Liam about that, I promised her soon.

"Girls, can you play with your toys in the living room for a bit while we finish up dinner?" I ask Ari.

She nods her head, then takes Kennedy's hand and skips to the living room.

Silence now sits in the air, and before I can break it, Liam speaks.

"I've uh, got something to take care of in my office. I'll be down before dinner."

He's gone before I can speak, and I'm left with whiplash. One minute, he's hot, the next, he's cold.

I shake my head and start to plate dinner. I'm waiting on the meatloaf to finish, and then we can eat. The entire time I'm making plates, I'm annoyed.

If he doesn't want to be around me, then why hire me as his nanny? Obviously, he's got his own issues to work through, but they haven't got a thing to do with me.

I sigh frustratedly and carry the plates to the table, calling for the girls. When I send Ari to get her dad, she comes back and says he will be here soon.

Liam joins us halfway through dinner, apologizing that he had a call that ran over. We eat in silence, aside from the girls' aimless chattering, and then I clean the dishes and put everything away. Since he's home tonight, it's essentially my night off. But the girls and I are falling into such a good routine, it feels weird not to give them a bath, brush their hair and get them all tucked in. Even if I've only been doing it for one week.

"Ari, don't pull on the shower curtain please," I hear Liam say from the bathroom, where he's sitting with the girls.

"Okay, Daddy! But you need to be the big guy with the hook!"

He sighs, and then she breaks out in song alongside Kennedy, giggling.

Maybe I could just pop in and see if he wants me to take over? I'm sure he has a lot of things to do after being on the road. He could relax.

I walk into the bathroom, and the girls squeal when they see me, bringing a smile to my face.

"Juliet! I am the princess of the water, just like Moana!" Ari says, splashing around in the shallow water. Ken giggles when the bubbles splash on her.

I walk closer to the bathtub and notice that Liam visibly stiffens the closer that I get. God, what's his problem?

"I was coming to check on the prettiest princesses there are. Want me to wash your hair?"

Liam stands up, "I've got this, Juliet. I'm home, therefore you don't have to do anything. I can handle this. Without you." His words are harsh. Whipping out and lashing me in the process.

I'm completely stunned. How can he be so sweet, gentle, and caring with the girls, but so cold and detached with me?

"I'm sorry, I just wanted to help." I glance at the girls who are playing quietly now, oblivious to the conversation.

"Well, I don't need your help right now. Thanks."

And just like that, I've been dismissed.

Like I'm not a person with feelings.

Fine.

I bite my lip, mulling over whether or not to tell him where he can stick it, but ultimately decide to leave. I turn on my heel and storm out of the room without another word. I'm scared that if I open my mouth right now, I'll say something I regret, or the tears that have begun to well behind my eyes will spill.

I don't give him that satisfaction. He doesn't deserve my tears.

I'll just take some time to myself, let the sting of his words fade, and take a hot bath to relax.

Maybe I'm just being sensitive? Maybe he had a long day, and he's taking it out on me unnecessarily. We've all had these days.

I walk upstairs and across the landing into my room, preparing all of my stuff for a hot bath, so I can get in there and get to bed early. I want to curl up with a good book before falling asleep. I haven't had time to read at all this week, and I am missing it.

Ooh, maybe something Alex recommended? Alley Ciz's new release sounds amazing. I pull my Kindle out and download it. The cover model is so hot.

Like most people, I definitely judge a book by its cover.

Since the girls are still bathing, I start reading on my Kindle, and the next thing I know, I'm waking with a start.

My face is numb. I apparently fell asleep with my face half pressed into my Kindle and half not. Stretching my arms over my head, I groan. God, I must have been so tired to pass out mid-read.

I get up from the bed and open the door slowly, pausing as it creaks, to find the hallway dark and quiet. Dang, it must be late. The girls are downstairs, but I still need to be quiet or I'll wake them. They're both such light sleepers. I tiptoe down the hallway towards the bathroom. When I pass by Liam's office, the door is slightly ajar, and the warm glow of his lamp casts light across the upstairs landing.

Because the door is slightly open, I can't help but overhear him on the phone. I don't intend to snoop or listen in on his conversation, but when I hear my name...my interest is piqued.

His deep, growly baritone rumbles through the door into the hallway, "Fuck off. Listen, she's my nanny. And as much as I'd rather not be around her, she's here to stay. The girls love her. I need her, and that's it. I need someone stable and present for the girls. You know I want them at home. I don't want them around media or any crazed fans." He pauses, "You know, Morris had a girl camped outside his house for a week? He finally got a restraining order. I'm not having my girls subjected to shit like that."

I suck in a sharp breath, the bitter sting of tears welling behind my eyes. That is the last thing I expect him to say, and I would be lying if I said it doesn't hurt.

That's how he feels?

"It is what it is. I'm staying away from her unless I have to, end of story. She'll be here for the girls."

He laughs at something, then agrees with whatever the person on the other end of the line says.

Wow. I shouldn't feel so...betrayed, but I do. I've been bursting with excitement for this job and doing the absolute best that I can, and this is how he's truly felt?

I wipe away the tears that have spilled hot and wet against my cheeks and walk to the bathroom, shutting the door quietly behind me.

You know what, fine. If this is how he wants to be—cold and

unfeeling—with me, for whatever reason, fine.

    At the end of the day, he's my employer.

    He's the boss. I'm the nanny.

    He's right.

    I'll stay out of his way and do my job.

    As far as I'm concerned, Liam Cartright can kiss my ass.

CHAPTER NINE
Liam

I love my job. I love this team. Hell, I love hockey. I always have.

But I miss my girls. God, I miss them. We've never been apart as much as we have in the past few weeks.

Seeing their faces over a screen at night is nowhere near the real thing. Even though I'm doing this for them at the same time as living out my own dreams, it doesn't make it any easier when it comes to saying goodbye.

So, when our PR director, Samantha, asks for a meeting with both Mark, the owner, and me... I'm eager to get it over with and head home to the girls.

I've been on the road, and the last thing I want to do is sit through a meeting, but seeing as how we aren't getting back to the rink until after seven, it must be time sensitive.

I put my bag in my office and head down to Mark's office at the end of the hallway. Samantha's waiting outside the closed door with a warm smile.

"Hi," she smiles.

I've only been here a short while, but I can tell that Sammy has her shit together. She keeps the guys on a short leash and doesn't put up with bullshit. Exactly what a group of oversized teenagers who think with their dicks ninety-nine percent of the time needs.

Being a new coach, I knew there would be kinks, and I'm sure that's why we're here tonight. Something's going on.

"Everything good?" I ask, shoving my hands in the pockets of my slacks.

She hesitates, "There's a situation I need to discuss with both you and Mark. I want to get ahead of it."

I nod.

Seconds later, Mark opens the door with a tired smile and gestures us in. "Thanks for setting this up Samantha, and for keeping me in the loop."

We take a seat at the large table in his office and wait while Samantha pulls her iPad out of her feminine briefcase.

Samantha's the kind of woman who eats you alive before you even realize she's the predator and you're the prey. She's always dressed to a T, in heels and pencil skirt, with her dark hair styled and makeup on. The woman is scary, and she wouldn't hesitate to pounce if needed, but from the exterior? You'd never know. She looks completely innocent, but I know better. I've seen it with my own eyes.

"It's not a secret that the best player on your team is also our biggest liability."

Her lips purse into a frustrated line.

Briggs Wilson.

Fuck, the kid is talented, I'll give him that. It's been a long time since I've seen someone move on the ice as fast, and as fluently, as he does. His stats are out of this world. He's without a doubt the best player on my team.

And he knows it. I haven't had much one-on-one time with him, but apparently, he's got some family shit going on and is determined to fuck up his life in the process.

"Wilson," I say gruffly.

"Yeah. It seems like every time I turn around, I'm having to clean up mess after mess. He says he's done with the partying, the public intoxication, the messy fights with his ex that involve the cops. But, on top of all of that, we have a new development."

Mark curses when she flips the iPad around to show us a website.

The top reads, "THE Puck Bunny," and it seems to be a gossip site centered around hockey. With the latest article being about Briggs and the PR nightmare that is his life.

She nods at the iPad, dark eyebrows raised, "This is a gossip site that sometimes reports stats, but it's mostly about the players and their personal lives. It's operated by someone anonymous, who calls herself "THE Puck Bunny", hence the title. And it seems like she's got her sights set on Briggs."

"Not like he isn't giving her plenty to report on."

"What makes this site any different from TMZ, or ESPN? There are plenty of sites out here that latch onto the guys," Mark asks, eyebrows raised in question.

"Well," Samantha sighs, "Several things. I wouldn't have brought it to either of you if I wasn't truly concerned. This girl has a massive following of loyal, pitch fork yielding fans. Even though no one knows who she is. Her fan base has insane reach. On all social platforms, she has millions of followers."

She scrolls with her bright red painted finger to show the other sites.

Holy fuck, *thirteen million* followers?

Samantha must read my expression because she laughs bitterly, "My thought as well. But the truth remains that she has the power to potentially hurt the team with her content. Not only does she seem hyper focused on Wilson for whatever reason, she's also got information that others haven't seemed to be able to obtain. I'm looking into that aspect."

Mark leans back in his chair and curses.

For a guy who is laid back and who has not once been remotely disheveled since I met him, he's looking a little alarming right now. His fists are clenched, and his face is red from anger. This is my first year coaching, the last thing I need is a scandal or to make headlines in any type of negative way.

Sam sighs and sits back in her chair before clasping her hands in front of her, "We've got to get it under control. Liam, this is where you step in and let him know that, essentially, if he doesn't get his shit together, he's off the team. Light the fire under his ass. Make him understand how serious this is. No more public escapades of any kind. Liam, this is a necessity. You're a new coach in the NHL and the team. Having a potential scandal could damage your career past repair."

If I have a player that has to be kicked off the team or traded due to misconduct, then Chicago won't be able to keep me as head coach, and the sad fact is, I may not be able to find another coaching position. Fuck, what kind of coach am I if I can't control my own players?

She's right, and it scares the fuck out of me. I need this job. I want this job. And I want to be damn good at it.

"I'm willing to do whatever it takes to make sure that it gets handled. Just tell me what you need from me."

"We need to work diligently, and start by bringing in Wilson for a conversation and letting him know the repercussions for his actions. Whatever is going on, he needs to seek professional help instead of spending his nights in bars. And...it's not just about Wilson. It's the entire team. We need *everyone* to keep their image clean, stay out of headlines, and walk the straight and narrow. We can't afford a mistake right now," she pauses, and pulls up another document on her iPad, then flips it around to us.

"I have a plan. Not gonna be easy, but with Puck Bunny determined to drag him even further through the mud, and with his destructive path, we've got to reshape his image. And fast."

"Whatever you need, you've got it."

The three of us get to work diving deep into Samantha's plan and determining how we are going to do what seems impossible. I don't want to lose Briggs, not by a long shot, but he can't bring the entire team down with him.

The next few weeks will be critical.

I slide my key in the deadbolt sometime after ten. The girls are probably tucked in bed, sound asleep but I couldn't wait to surprise them in the morning with breakfast at their favorite diner, The Pancake House. I feel like every time I'm away, I have to make up for the time we lost.

When I travel with the team, I pack light, so the only luggage I have is my old high school hockey duffle back.

If anything, I'm a sentimental asshole. I shut the door behind me then set my bag on the floor next to the door before I walk to the alarm and disarm it.

Good, I'm glad she's not forgetting to set it at night. It's one of those things I'm anal over, as Shana likes to say.

And surprisingly, Juliet hasn't had much to say to me since she moved in. It's like the night after she got here, something shifted. I didn't know what. She was polite, but to the point. Colder to me, but warm and open with the girls. Movie night, she shifted as far away from me as possible. Avoids me in the house at all costs.

I didn't want things to be awkward, but this was how it had to be. I had to keep my distance and her at arm's length.

At least that's what I keep telling myself. It's easier to lie and pretend that I don't have some crazy attraction to my nanny.

Sounds better in my head too.

I sigh, and walk into the kitchen to grab a drink before I hit the shower and get into bed. I want to wake the girls up early so we can get breakfast. It feels fucking good to be home. It's been a long time since I've had to be on the road this much, and I forget how much of a toll it takes on you. Body and mind.

Despite being on the road most of the day and the meeting with Sam and Mark, I'm wide awake. Pretty sure I'm running on adrenaline alone. Which means that I probably won't be going to bed until I hit the gym…. or relieve some tension another way.

Fuck.

I curse inwardly and groan, my mind immediately flashing to Juliet and the way her hips swayed in that dress she wore to her interview. Tight and hugging her lithe body, I could've pulled her against me and kissed her breathless then. Maybe Reed was right, maybe it is time to start putting myself out there or at least find a casual hookup who understands that I want nothing beyond that.

My problem isn't finding someone to get lost in, it's finding a woman who interests me or my dick enough. I take my water that I swiped from the fridge and head upstairs to my office. I guess if I can't sleep, I'll work on some shit I've been putting off on the computer. The sky has opened up outside, thunder and lightning and the wind whipping, therefore going for a run outside is out of the question, so I guess I'll skip the gym and look over the stuff Samantha sent with me. Some PR events we need to get Briggs into.

When I make it to the top of the landing, I see the bathroom light on and the warm glow of light casting from under the threshold. Juliet's on the other side of that door, probably wet.... and naked, soapy...

I squeeze my eyes shut and then shake my head as if it'll remove the mental picture from my thoughts and go to my office. I shut the door behind me and flop down onto my desk chair before sighing.

What the hell are you doing Liam?

The last thing I needed was to get caught up in this. I finally found someone capable of caring for my children and now I have a raging hard on when she's in the vicinity, great.

First of all, I needed to stop thinking about her. Period. I open my email and look at the list of events Samantha emailed over. The first one on the list is the Children's Hospital and that's always a great place to be. He can take pictures with the kids, do face painting. Hell, dress his ass up in some costume to make them laugh, I don't give a shit.

He had a lot of work to do and if he isn't going to put in the effort, he'd be off the team. Simple as that. I was willing to do whatever it took to see him succeed. He's my player, and I believe that underneath all of this acting out shit, he had something good inside. He's a great kid.

I used to be him. The guy everyone loved, the life of any and every party, the guy who had puck bunnies lined up down the hall, and then I realized how fast I would drive my career in the ground by not focusing on hockey.

A loud clap of thunder sounds outside, so close that the glass on the bay window rattles against the frame. It's followed by the crack of lightning, and then the power flicks, and my office goes dark. Shit, the power's out from the storm.

Suddenly, a blood curdling scream comes from what seems like the bathroom and I leap from the chair, almost tripping over a Barbie in the middle of the floor, and thrust my door open, running down the landing to the guest bathroom.

I don't even knock, I just sling the door open and rush inside, colliding with Juliet in the process. Her soft body lands against mine with so much force, it knocks me into the door and it shuts with a loud thud.

"Ow. Shit!" She curses, one hand clutching her head that connected with my chest and the other clutching the tiniest white towel around her body. The only light in the room comes from a small window above the tub that casts pale, silvery moonlight against her already milky white skin that's on full display.

Jesus *Christ*.

"What happened? Are you alright?" I ask, desperately trying to keep my eyes from dropping to her chest that's all but spilling from the towel. Trying and failing. She obviously wrapped it around herself in a hurry, but in doing so, must have grabbed an oversized hand towel instead of an actual towel. Steam billows between us as the shower continues to spray, scorchingly hot beyond the curtain. It's thick in the air between us, palpable like the tension. There's hardly room between us in the small bathroom.

My back's pressed against the door, and she's standing mere inches away still glistening with the reminisce of her shower. Entirely fucking inappropriate, but goddamn I don't make a move to leave.

"I.. The thunder- it.. I'm so sorry. I was showering and the lightning struck and then it went dark. I was scared."

Her bottom lip trembles slightly and she looks on the verge of tears. Obviously, storms are something she's terrified of. Without thinking, I reach out and run my thumb along her jaw absentmindedly, meant to calm her.

"Hey, it's fine. The power just went off from the storm."

She looks up at the same time her breath hitches, and we both realize that my hands are on her, and neither of us have pulled away. If anything, I think she might press closer, sinking into my touch.

I should stop. Move away. Put as much distance as I can between the two of us.

But, fuck she's so gorgeous I feel stuck. My feet are permanently a part of this tile floor beneath me. Her eyes are wide, pools of honey that I want to fucking drown in. The sweetest death there could be.

Her chest rises and falls in shallow dips and I know she's as turned on right now as I am. It would only take one simple flick of my wrist and the towel would fall in a puddle at her feet, leaving her bare for me. My eyes drop to her throat where her pulse pounds wildly against her pale skin, and it takes every ounce of restraint I have not to drop my lips to the slope of her neck. Fresh out of the shower she smells like the tangy sweet scent of peach and orange mixed. I don't know what she uses, but it was quickly becoming my favorite scent in the world.

I lean in closer and inhale, watching as her eyes dilate with need, and I'm seconds away from giving in and saying fuck it. Fuck the consequences.

Her fists are clenched tightly in the towel but she lets go slightly, letting it drop a hair of an inch before she catches it with the other hand.

"Liam..." She breathes, her hand traveling up to mine that's cradling her jaw with my thumb still grazing her skin in a calming motion. "What are we doing?"

Her question is one I don't have an answer to, but I do know that I don't want to stop. Whatever it is, I don't want it to end. I want to stay inside this bubble, just the two of us, high on the feeling that I'm experiencing right now.

"I-" I clear my throat that's hoarse with need, "I don't know Juliet." And I don't. This is unchartered fucking territory. All I know is that there's nothing I want more than to take her against this door until she's hoarse from her cries.

She nods, understanding exactly what I mean without having to elaborate.

My head drops lower, closer and closer to her lips. I can practically taste her against my tongue, and I haven't even kissed her. Slowly, we move, ready to meet in the middle. Her hand tightens around mine at her jaw. A second more and she'll be fucking mine.

"Juliet?" Ari's voice comes from the other side of the door in a watery cry, "I'm scared and my night light went off."

We break apart so quickly, some of her towel slips and I get a glimpse of her chest. Her tits are perfect, round, high and pert with rosy peaks. Hard little nubs that beg for my mouth. Goddamnit.

"Juliet. I need you to cover up and walk out of this bathroom before we do something that we cannot come back from." My voice comes out scratchy at best. She hesitates, pulling her lip into her mouth before nodding and reaching behind her for another towel. I look away as she secures it around her, and then she brushes past me and opens the door, slipping out. I hear her talking to Ari then the stairs creak as they walk down together.

I don't know what the fuck just happened, but I think it might have just changed everything.

CHAPTER TEN
Juliet

Days later, and I still can't stop thinking about Liam and how it felt with him in that bathroom. I can't believe he saw me half-naked, or that we almost crossed a line. And had Ari not interrupted us...I think we might have. We seem to be stuck in a limbo, both of us teetering towards the edge of nothing remaining the same, but never fully crossing.

I'm getting whiplash in the process.

Regardless, now I'm left frustrated and confused by his hot and cold demeanor. What's worse is, despite any of those things, I have this attraction to him that makes my thighs clench in anticipation whenever he walks through the door.

I blame my body. What a traitor she is.

Now, he's home for the next three days, and I'm not sure how things will be between us. But I guess they can't be any more tense than when he's cold and unfriendly towards me. Add in a side of awkwardness, and it'll be great. One minute, there seems to be this undeniable, sizzling tension between us. A tautness that feels tangible whenever we're together. The next, it's like water dousing a raging flame. He becomes stoic and distant, completely shutting me out.

He left a note this morning to let me know that he and the girls were going out for breakfast and that they'd be back later. So, that bought me time. But I hear the front door slam, and now I have to face him. It's time. We live in the same house, and I'm his daughters' nanny.

Even if I'd rather hide in here all day than see him again.

Get it together Juliet. It was an almost kiss that meant nothing. People almost kiss all the time. And he barely saw your entire boob. No big deal. You'll just pretend it never happened and go on with your day.

Okay, that is a pep talk fail. Now I feel even worse.

I take another deep breath before gathering my courage and joining them downstairs.

The second Ari sees me round the corner, she's darting from her chair and colliding with me. Ken follows right behind her, and they are a flurry of energy and excitement as they hug onto any part of me they can grab.

"Juliet, guess what! Daddy took us to the Farmers Market! We got to get so many new fruits!" Ari says so quickly she's out of breath by the time she finishes. My eyes lift to find Liam staring at me intently. When our eyes connect, he looks away and busies himself with his book on the counter.

Okay...maybe as awkward as I thought.

"That's awesome! I'm so glad you got to spend time together. What do you guys plan to do with the rest of your day?" I ask.

Liam looks up at us before clearing his throat. He's obviously flustered and it's almost... cute. A big, surly guy like him flustered. Maybe our almost kiss affected him the same way that it has me. Not that he'll ever admit it, but...It still makes me feel slightly better.

"Uh, so the girls and I are going to go ice skating today. If you'd uh, like to join us. No big deal if not..."

Wait, he's inviting me to come? I pause for a moment and mull over his words. I don't want to intrude on their private time or make things more awkward for him...or me.

With what just happened, should I really spend more time around Liam? It seems impossible to have a conversation with him that isn't only politeness.

"Juliet, you have to come watch me do a twirl! Daddy said that if I keep it up, he will put me in ice skating classes."

"Me too!" Ken squeals.

The girls both convince me to say yes because, at the end of the day, I want to spend time with them, even if it means a day with Liam and his broody jerk self.

"Okay, okay. I'll come. I haven't been since I was about your age, Ari. Let me grab my bag?"

Liam nods as Ari and Ken jump up and down in excitement.

"Daddy says my twirl is the most beautiful-ist he's seen!" Ari practices a few spins where she bounces into the wall with her over-abundance of energy.

"I have no doubt that you will be the prettiest princesses on the ice!" I tell them both, giving them a quick squeeze before releasing them. "Let me grab my stuff, and I'll be right back."

I head back upstairs and grab my coat, scarf and a pair of thick socks. If my memory serves right, your toes are generally iced over afterwards, so maybe this will help. When I go back downstairs, both girls are dressed in matching sweatsuits, with pink glittery scarves wrapped around their necks.

They look adorable. My gaze flits to Liam, who sees the smile on my lips and shrugs before opening the door and leading us outside. He might be a jerk sometimes, but he's a great father, and these girls are lucky to have him.

I sit in the passenger seat of Liam's SUV on the way to the rink, and there's a thick, heavy tension that sits in the air between us. He keeps his eyes trained on the road, while I watch the city pass through the window. Even though I shouldn't, I sneak a glance or two as he drives, and I can't help but notice the way his hands grip the steering wheel, strong and unwavering, the muscles of his biceps straining against the Henley he has on.

Obviously, I'm sexually frustrated, and it doesn't help that the man I'm forced to live with is the cause of it, or that he's ridiculously handsome and completely forbidden.

"Juliet?"

"Hmm?" I rip my eyes from his hands and drag them to his eyes instead. His brow is furrowed, and from the small, smug grin that sits on his lips, I know I've been caught…admiring.

"Sorry, what did you say?"

"We're here."

My cheeks immediately flame with embarrassment, and I pray that he can't see the pink on my cheeks. God, I have to get a grip.

Liam parks his SUV in front of a large white building that has seen better days. The paint is peeling and cracking, and the sign looks like it might fall at any moment. It's in desperate need of an update. I'm kind of surprised Liam's brought us here, when he's a professional hockey coach and probably has access to state-of-the-art facilities. Maybe it's presumptuous of me to assume that.

"I can practically hear you thinking from over here," Liam laughs as we walk through the parking lot to the entrance. The door creaks loudly as he opens it and holds it so we can walk ahead of him.

"Just…observing," I say.

The inside is no different from the outside, but it feels… welcoming. Even though it's not fancy or over the top, it's simple and cozy.

"This place was built in nineteen seventy-four. This is the place I laced my first pair of skates. Where I learned to skate, where I learned how to play hockey. I spent more nights here with a stick, a puck, and a goal than I did at home growing up. It was my second home."

Now it makes sense. This place is familiar for Liam. He's been coming here his entire life.

I look at the girls skipping ahead of us to the rental booth, holding hands and giggling, "So…you've been bringing the girls here. Just like you, right?"

He nods, "I'm sentimental about this place. It just feels right to bring my girls here to experience the same things I did as a kid. They both love it here. The owner, Tom, is a good friend. We try to make it here at least twice a month, depending on my schedule. But we haven't been in a while, since I've been on the road. It also helps that it's private, and no media is allowed here. It's not that

way at the arena. The girls' privacy is important to me."
I can't believe he's actually...volunteering information about himself. Even about something small. After the first conversation we had, he's been completely standoffish.

When we get to the rental counter, Liam takes the lead and orders skates for himself and the girls, then he looks at me.

Right, he wouldn't know my skate size.

"Uhm, I need a six, please. Thank you." I tell the teenager behind the counter.

Once he hands them over, I help the girls lace up their skates and then put on mine. The second I stand, wobbly and off balance, I start to regret my decision to join them. I haven't been ice skating since I was a child, and I'm pretty sure it's not like riding a bike and something I'll pick right back up.

Actually, I'm pretty sure I'll end up in a heap in the middle of the ice, and that won't be embarrassing...at all. Especially not surrounded by an ex-professional hockey player who can skate circles around me in his sleep.

I groan inwardly. I'm beginning to sound like Gladys when she's obsessing over her latest boy toy at Everwood.

Ari and Kennedy sashay up, each take one of my hands, and drag me towards the large rink. It's as big as a football field, or at least, it feels that way when I'm standing here, about to take my first step onto the ice. Liam goes first and skates ahead of us, and for the first time...I get to see him in action. What I don't expect is how effortless and natural he is as he glides on each skate, barreling forward.

Wow.

Without a doubt, Liam Cartright must have been an amazing

hockey player. There's no way he wasn't, with that kind of natural ability.

I make a mental note to go full Alex and look up old videos of him during his days as a player. Now, I'm anxious to see him with a stick in hand. Even though he's over six feet tall with a body of solid muscle, he moves so gracefully. It's as if his feet barely touch the ice. His movements are fluid, strong, and controlled. Much like him as a person.

Liam is disciplined in a way that most people wish to be. I've seen him wake up at five every morning that he's home and push his body to the limit in the gym while his girls are still asleep. He keeps a strict schedule with the girls, from what they eat to the amount of time they're allowed on their tablets.

But here, on the ice? He's different. There's an ease about him that I've never seen. I guess this is the environment that he feels most comfortable in. Without the worry of fans or media and paparazzi, he can spend time with his girls and do something they enjoy together.

Speaking of the girls…they've abandoned ship and joined Liam out on the ice. Their matching sweatsuits, paired with the furry pom pom beanies, are so cute it tugs a string inside my heart. What's even more shocking is that Kennedy, at three years old, stepped right out onto the ice and is currently skating circles around Liam.

I'm going to get shown up by a three-year-old.

Pretty sure if Nana was here, she'd tell me to stop being a puss, so here we go.

The second the blade of my skate hits the ice, my ankle shakes, and my hand flies out to catch the side of the wall and keep me upright.

One foot - check.

Ari and Kennedy are giggling a few feet in front of me as Liam pretends to do ballerina moves on the ice, and as he twirls, they mimic him.

I mean, it can't be that hard, right? If a three-year-old and five-year-old can do it, then I can do it.

My false bravado almost lands me on my ass when I take another step with my right foot and step fully on to the slick ice. If it wasn't for the fact that it'll be even more embarrassing to say I chickened out of skating, I would be over at the concession stand getting hot chocolate and watching the girls be brave.

Come on, Juliet.

I exhale a deep breath and gently glide my foot forward. When I do, I go much further than intended, and the safety of the wall is gone, leaving me a wobbling, unsteady mess on the ice.

"Maybe I should sit this one out. It's been a while..." I say to Liam. He's doing his best not to laugh, which is good, because I'm not responsible for what will happen if he does. The girls are holding hands with him, skating circles and figure eights, and I'm stock still in fear that I might topple over.

"No Juliet, you have to come with us!" Ari cries. She looks on the verge of tears, and then I feel bad.

"Okay, I just have to go slow, girls." I croak.

Did I mention I'm seriously regretting this decision?

Just checking.

Much like a newborn baby foal, my legs are trembling the second I try to glide forward. My hands immediately reach out to grab on to something, but the wall is no longer here, and I'm grasping at empty air.

Just as I'm about to hit the ice, Liam is there, yanking me up by the elbow. I crash into him so hard we both almost topple over, and I mutter a curse.

Shit.

"I'm so sorry."

One move and I'm going down, and without an ounce of grace.

"You okay?" Liam asks, not bothering to hide his amusement.

I suppress a grimace, "Fine. Just a little out of practice, that's all."

And completely embarrassed. I'm literally the most uncoordinated, clumsy person on the planet. The last place I should be is an ice skating rink in a pair of skates that are clearly going to send me to my ass. I once broke a toe from running into...the wall.

That's the kind of person I am. So, ice skating hasn't been very high on my to do list. Most sports or physical activities where I can end up hurt are actually pretty low on my list.

My eyes flit to the girls, and I'm still amazed at how easily they move on the ice. I guess that's what happens when your dad is a retired NHL player and the coach of one of the best teams in the country. The ice is second nature for both Liam and the girls. They've been raised on the ice.

Ari spins in a circle and calls out to me, "Juliet, come on! Twirl like a princess with me and Ken! Pleaseeeee!"

Just the movement makes my head spin. I absolutely bit off way more than I could chew tonight.

"Take your time. Do you want me to get you some crates so you can hold on to them?"

I look around and see there are a few younger kids who have

stacked up milk crates on the ice, and they're pushing them around to help keep their balance.

"Uh, no…I'll be fine. Go skate with the girls."

He nods before skating off to join the girls. I'm so busy focusing on the way the muscles in his back move as he skates and how his pants show off just how tight and firm his butt is, that I don't even notice the patch of slick ice ahead of me until the front of my skate hits it. Then, in what feels like slow motion, my feet come out from under me, and I'm falling on my ass. Hard.

I land on my ankle, and it makes a strange pop. Suddenly, the pain radiates up my leg, and tears immediately sting, hot and watery behind my eyes.

Holy. Hell.

Well…this officially just became the worst idea I've ever had, and I have a feeling it's about to get worse.

CHAPTER ELEVEN
Juliet

My ankle is hurting so bad that I hardly have time to think about the fact that I just busted my ass in front of Liam and made a complete fool of myself.

Okay, that's a lie. Not only does my ankle feel like it just broke in half, I'm also embarrassed beyond belief.

God, if you're listening…feel free to put me out of my misery.

"Shit, Juliet, are you okay?" Liam croaks as he skates up and drops to his knees in front of me.

I shake my head, "Uh, my ankle hurts. Bad. Like…really bad." I sniffle, "I think I sprained it. I wasn't paying attention, I…I…I was just distracted."

Distracted ogling Liam's butt. Only I would potentially break a limb because of a pair of tight buns. Wait till Nana hears about this. I'll never live it down.

Ari and Kennedy appear beside us, and they drop down next to me, each of them a teary mess. Kennedy's wild curls fall in her face as she reaches out to wrap her tiny arms around me.

It's comfort that I didn't realize how badly I needed right now. The love of these girls.

"Are you okay, Juliet? Do you have a booboo?" Ari whispers. Her bright blue eyes are filled with tears, and I realize they're probably worried, since they all witnessed my fall.

I give her a forced smile, even though the throbbing pain in my ankle brings tears to my eyes once more.

Shit, this is bad. I might have actually broken it. Not that I want to try, but I doubt I can even move it, and the pain radiating all the way down to my toes has me slightly freaking out.

"We need to get your skates off and look at it. You need to see a doctor and have it checked out." Liam says.

No, no, no.

And let Liam see I don't have health insurance? No, absolutely not.

I force another smile, and put on my false bravado, "I'm fine really, it's probably just a bruise. I'll get an ice pack and it'll be okay. Trust me. I'm such a klutz—this is nothing new."

Except the pain in my ankle says differently.

Liam squints, looking at me incredulously before shaking his head, "You're not fine. I can see the pain on your face. You're hurt, Juliet."

Before I can even respond, he's picking me up like I weigh nothing at all, bridal style. Even with a hurt ankle, I can't deny my body's response to him. His hands wrap around the backs of my thighs in a tight grip, and he skates towards the exit with ease. Ari and Kennedy trail closely behind us.

"You don't have to carry me. I can walk," I protest. My protest seems weak, even to my own ears.

He only shakes his head, "Looks like it."

Jerk.

I mutter to myself, but obviously he hears because the corner of his lip curves up in a small smile.

"I'm perfectly capable of walking. It's just a…little sprain," I try again.

Wincing, I try and wiggle it back and forth, but the pain shoots up my leg in bolts. Okay, maybe it's a little worse than I'm willing to let on.

It's embarrassing, falling on your ass, in front of everyone. Especially the man you have been lusting after, and who you almost had a thing with in the bathroom two days ago. And now, he's having to carry me through the building. Admittedly, I want his hands on me, but not because I'm a klutz and hurt myself—because he wants to.

Once we're off the ice, Liam gently sets me down on the bleacher bench next to the rink and begins to unlace his skates. He makes quick work of his, then moves on to the girls while I watch.

His biceps flex under his dark green Henley, and his brow furrows in concentration as he works.

"Juliet, are you going to be okay?" Ari cries. Her bottom lip trembles as she walks next to her daddy, hand in hand with Ken. They both look so upset, my heart squeezes.

"I'm okay, sweet girl, it's just a little booboo on my ankle. I'll be ready to play again soon."

I reach out and stroke her cheek, and she seems to accept my answer, for now.

Once he's done situating the girls and getting their shoes on, Liam kneels back down in front of me. His hair is longer than usual, and it falls into his eyes. My ankle screams in protest when he gingerly picks my foot up and starts to unlace my skate. I bite back the tears and try not to draw attention to the fact that it hurts so badly, but I completely fail when the tears spill over.

"You don't have to pretend with me, Juliet." His voice is gruff, and it hits me directly in the heart. The words mean more than just the injury, and the way his eyes flash, he knows it.

The dangerous, illicit waters that we continue to wade through, despite the repercussions that could come.

Liam is my boss. He's off limits. But...tell my heart that. Convince my body not to be set afire the second his smoldering eyes meet mine.

Somehow, my thoughts distract me from his actions, and he gets my skate off, then peels the fuzzy sock down my foot, revealing a very swollen and angry red ankle.

"Shit, Juliet," he curses, shaking his head. The coarse pads of his fingers brush lightly against the top of my ankle, and he presses tenderly against my swollen flesh. "You need a doctor to look at this. I've seen a ton of injuries in my career, and I know when a doctor is needed. I have a friend who does some sports medicine work. I'll call him. He can come to the house."

My chest sags in relief. No hospitals mean no bills.

I nod, "Thank you, Liam."

His eyes hold mine, and something passes between us. Another moment that feels like...more. Yet, as quickly as it happens, it's gone. He clears his throat and begins removing my other skate. The way he so tenderly handles me causes my throat to clog with emotion.

"I'm going to carry you to the car, and you're not going to say a word. You're hurt, and you're going to hurt yourself more if you try to walk on it."

This time, I don't bother with faux protests.

Who knew that something so innocent as the feeling of my foot in Liam's strong hands could feel so...erotic? The way his fingers delicately brush against my skin, sending a shiver down my spine.

He's entirely too good with his fingers. Which makes me think of what else he can do with them...

Oh God, I'm injured and still thinking about Liam when that's what got me into trouble in the first place.

I'm sitting on the couch with my foot propped in his lap as he inspects it. Dark purple bruises have already begun to bloom under the skin of my ankle, and each time he rubs his thumb lightly across the arch of my foot, I shudder.

It hurt as he assessed the damage, but it seems like, with each swipe of his finger, the pain dissipates. My eyes scan his face and drink in his handsome features while he works. His eyes, dark gray-green flecked, scan my foot. He's so focused, his brow furrowed, and his jaw tight. I jerk when he presses hard against the sole of my foot, and he mutters an apology.

"You seem to know a lot about injuries," I say.

He shrugs, "Had enough injuries in my career that I learned enough to take care of stuff myself. Hockey's brutal." He pauses, looking down at my foot in his lap, "I think it's only sprained, but Chris will be able to tell us for sure."

I nod, biting my lip and sinking further into the couch. This is weird. Liam being gentle and, I don't know...tentative with me. I've seen it countless times with the girls, but to have it directed at me is different. It causes flutters in the pit of my stomach, and I know that I shouldn't read into this. He's doing what he thinks is right.

Especially after what happened in the bathroom, I'm treading carefully. I don't want him to shut down and push me away again, but he can't deny that there's something between us. Something that is simmering and bubbling to the top.

"I'm going to situate the girls before Chris gets here. Just call my name if you need anything. Here's a few pain killers until he gets here." He lifts my foot carefully off his lap and places it on the pillows he's propped up, then grabs the glass of water off the side table and hands it to me, along with two small pills.

My fingers brush against his palm as I pick up the pills, then take them with the glass of water. His eyes meet mine, and he looks away before setting the water down and leaving.

Suddenly, I'm embarrassed and feeling guilty that I've put a damper on their entire day. The girls were so looking forward to ice skating, and now Liam is giving me all of his attention. I'll have to make it up to them.

Maybe we'll go for ice cream, and it can be our little secret.

While waiting for Liam's friend to arrive, I must have dozed off because I feel a hand on my arm, shaking me awake. My eyes open, groggily, and I see Liam and a blonde guy dressed in slacks and a polo standing over me.

I try to sit up, but Liam stops me before I can, "This is my buddy, Chris. He's been fixing me up since we were kids."

Chris extends his hand for me to shake, "I'm Chris. I'm just going to take a look at your ankle and see what we're working with."

He quickly inspects my foot and then looks at me, "Yeah, looks like a pretty nasty sprain. You need to keep it elevated and ice it every few hours to reduce the swelling. Take anti-inflammatories and rest. Stay off of it for the next week or so, and you should be good to go."

Liam thanks him and shakes his hand again, and then he's gone as quickly as he came.

"Wow, that was pain free."

"Yeah, Chris is a good guy. I'm glad it's not broken."

"Me too."

He sits down at the end of the couch and picks my foot up again, placing it back into his lap while he gets to work with the wrap that Chris left. The tips of his fingers skim across the arch of my foot, to the sole, over to the top where the dark bruises are marring my skin. Featherlight swipes of his thumb have my core clenching.

God, all the man has to do is touch me and I'm a pile of mush.

He quickly and delicately wraps my foot, then puts the ice on top where the bruising is the worst.

His eyes drag up to meet mine, and my breath hitches. He's so unbelievably handsome. It's unfair for someone to be so effortlessly attractive. It's easy to get lost in the depth of his eyes, easy to get lost in Liam. That's the problem. This unexplainable draw I feel to him? It's more than physical.

Liam is dangerously handsome, and absolutely forbidden. If I'm not careful, I'm going to get hurt. That much I know. But…it didn't stop the pull I have to him. It's magnetic, and I know that I can't stop it. I've tried. To turn off these feelings, and push them away.

I guess for Liam, it's easier. The hot and cold demeanor is his defense mechanism. His way of protecting his own heart.

If only I had any defenses for my heart.

CHAPTER TWELVE
Liam

The girls have officially made Juliet their patient.

In the last two days, they've checked her "temperature" with the plastic thermometer that Kennedy got in her doctor kit during Christmas at least a hundred times. Not only have the doting nurses taken her temp, but they've checked her blood pressure and left Princess Sparkles for moral support.

And even though her ankle is swollen and bruised to hell and back, Juliet has been the best sport. She told me to leave the girls alone and let them be, and that she needed her nurses.

I've just put the girls down to bed, and I'm going back to the couch to check on her. She's been there since she injured her foot because there's no way she's making it up the stairs, and chances are...she'll just end up hurting herself further. So, between the girls and me, we've been taking care of her.

When I walk back into the living room, she's sitting on the couch with one leg tucked under her while her foot is propped up. Even though she's got a set of crutches, she's right when she said she's clumsy.

That's the understatement of the damn century. I've caught her twice in the past two days as she hobbles around the house when I'm not looking.

"Liam?"

"Yeah?"

She looks up at me through thick lashes, "Um...so, I know this is totally inappropriate, and I'm sorry to even ask but...I need to shower. Can you possibly help me wrap my foot so it doesn't get wet?"

My mind immediately goes to the other day in the bathroom when she dropped her towel. Fuck, it's all I've been able to think about since it happened. The sweet peaks of her nipples that I want to devour until they're swollen and she's writhing against me.

The exact thing I shouldn't be thinking of. Which is why I've kept my distance...until now.

"Yeah, of course. Let me grab a bag."

I leave her on the couch and quickly grab a bag from the closet. It's going to take every bit of strength I possess to keep my thoughts from the other night, but I can't fuck everything up.

Not when so much is on the line.

Not when it would change everything.

"Ready?" I ask, holding up the bag.

She nods, so I carefully pick her foot up and begin securing the bag over it, tying it as tightly as I can without hurting her to prevent any water getting on her wrap. Once I'm done, I set her foot down, and she grabs her crutches.

Wobbling, she stands with the assistance of the crutches, but her foot catches the edge of the coffee table and she almost falls.

"Damnit," she curses.

It's fucking adorable. She's so frustrated that she's restricted in her ability to move, she uses her other foot and kicks the coffee table.

"I'm so tired of not being able to do anything myself."

"I can help you. It's no big deal. And the girls have toys everywhere in their bathroom, so you can use mine for now."

Get it together Liam, your words are garbled, and you sound like an idiot.

Her cheeks flush in embarrassment, "I would appreciate it. I'm scared I'll end up with another injury if I'm left alone to do it." She laughs, and I shake my head.

She's right.

I stoop down, and she wraps her arm around my neck so I can support her as we walk to the master bathroom. Once we get inside, she leans against the counter for support while I turn on the shower.

"Hot? Warm?"

"Uh, hot please. As hot as it goes."

I turn the dial all the way up and close the glass door.

"Thank you for the past few days, Liam. I know taking care of someone else wasn't your plan, and I'm sorry for that, but thank you. I truly appreciate it."

"It's no problem at all. I'll uh, leave you to it, then. I'm going to stay in my room in case you need anything."

Juliet nods and gives me a smile. One that hits me in the gut like a punch. She's so damn beautiful...she's completely intoxicating. One taste, and I'd be gone. I walk out of the bathroom like it's on fire and shut the door behind me.

This is what we need. A barrier between us. And I'm not going to think about her on the other side of that door, naked and wet, running the loofah down her slick and soapy body to the delicate juncture of her thighs.

I'm not.

My dick doesn't get the memo, though, and I'm about to bust a hole through my gym shorts. Damnit.

I sit on the bed and grab the remote, turning on the latest hockey game and focusing my attention only on the tv, not letting my mind wander. After a few minutes, I hear a loud thud, and then seconds later, I hear Juliet call out for me.

Shit, did she fall in the shower?

I'm out of the bed in seconds and burst through the door into the bathroom. As soon as I open the door, steam immediately hits me in the face. Hot and sticky, it's heavy in the air.

"Juliet, are you okay? What happened?"

My eyes dart to the shower, and see the glass is completely fogged, but I can still make out the silhouette of Juliet's shapely figure in a heap on the floor.

Damnit, Juliet.

"Uh…I sort of fell. Um, and now I can't get back up. The handle is too far for me to reach."

I squeeze my eyes shut, and I breathe for a second. I think the devil is actually tempting my life right about now, and fuck…I'm not as strong as I thought.

"Okay, I'm going to open the door and come in. I'll close my eyes."

"Okay." she whispers.

When I close my hand around the handle and yank open the

door, I advert my eyes from Juliet, but still reach down to help her off the floor. She clutches my arm in earnest, and finally, she's back on her feet. Her hands fist into my shirt unsteadily, and then she catapults into me. Suddenly, we're both under the hot spray. Water pours down my face, and my eyes fly open when she squeaks. I grasp onto her back to keep her from falling, and then I realize...

Juliet is naked and pressed against me. In the shower, while the hot water soaks us both.

This is fucking bad. No, actually it's worse than bad.

"Liam," she breathes. Water clings to her lashes, and she gazes up at me with those big, honey eyes. Her chest is pressed against me. We're completely molded together, and I can feel her everywhere.

I'm only so strong, and I've officially reached my fucking limit.

I slam my mouth onto hers, sucking in that lip that has driven me crazy for the entire time she's been here. She moans against my mouth and slides her hands up to wind her fingers into my hair. When I tease the seam of her lips with my tongue, her hands fist in my hair, and I know that she is as desperate for me as I am for her.

I rip my lips from hers and kiss away the droplets of water on her neck, lower and lower until I reach her breasts, then I suck her nipple into my mouth. She cries out, throwing her head back and chanting my name as I finally have it my fucking way and worship the hardened rosy peaks that have haunted my nightmares since the first night I saw them.

Juliet has the most perfect tits I've ever seen. They're perfect handfuls, and fuck, they look like they were made just for my hands.

I lower myself to my knees before her as I kiss a path down her slick body, using my tongue to dip inside her belly button as I make it to the flare of her hips. I nip at her hip bone and kiss the indent of skin at her hip. Her body is fucking perfect. Hell, Juliet is perfect.

I know I should stop, and she should stop me. But, right now, I can't think of anything other than the taste of Juliet on my tongue. I'm desperate for it.

Finally, I make it to the mound of her pussy, and I drag my lips along the sensitive flesh. My hand travels up the back of her thighs, lifting her hurt leg off the ground and placing it on my shoulders. Her hands fist in my hair as she holds on, still remaining upright. Lifting her leg up spreads her wide, and I suck in a sharp hiss.

Fuck, her pussy is beautiful. Pink and pouty. Her clit is a small bundle of nerves that I can't wait to devour. I don't waste another second not having my mouth on her, and I flatten my tongue against her pussy, licking from her tight hole to her clit.

She bucks against me, almost yanking out my hair, but fuck, it makes me even more starved for her taste. I close my mouth around her clit and suck, rolling the little nub between my lips, and she writhes violently against my mouth.

"Liam," my name is a short panting moan from her lips. One I want to hear for the rest of my damn life.

I take my time feasting on her pussy, inhaling her scent. I've wanted this, wanted her, for so long, it feels like I'm finally unwrapping a gift. And when I slide my middle fingers inside of her tight, dripping heat, she falls apart against my tongue. Over and over, she rides my face as the orgasm consumes her.

If we weren't in the damn shower, I'd sit on the floor so she could really ride me.

"Oh God," she whispers, once it's over. I pull myself off the floor and hold onto her because she's spineless right now, and she squeezes her eyes shut. "So, that just happened." She laughs nervously.

It did.

And as much as I wanted it, and would give practically anything to have it happen again, it shouldn't have.

We crossed a line tonight, and I don't know what will happen, but right now? I'm not even fucking thinking about it.

I want to savor the taste of Juliet on my tongue.

CHAPTER THIRTEEN
Juliet

I never really considered myself a hockey fan. Or a fan of any sports, honestly. So, really, I know a grand total of two things about hockey as a whole.

1) You skate on ice with a stick and a puck.

2) You try to hit said puck into the goal. Which one? Not sure. One of them, though.

I never really understood people's absolute devotion to sports or the players, but slowly...I'm learning what it means.

Starting with having no less than a hundred people in Liam's backyard for a team BBQ. Players, their families, and their children will all be here in the next couple of hours.

Logically, I shouldn't be stressed, but I am so stressed. Not that Liam went out of his way to say it, but I can tell it's important to him. This is his first year as coach, and he's desperately trying to get to know his players and make them feel whole as a team.

So, I've made every side I can possibly think of because I hear that athletes have big appetites, and if they eat anything like Liam... the last thing we want to do is run out of food.

"Juliet, can I please, please have one of these?" Ari begs from the table, where she's eyeing a petite sandwich with hungry eyes.

Did I say athletes eat a lot? I'm obviously mistaken because toddlers eat even more.

"One. And not another. We have to save these for all of your daddy's guests!" I laugh and shake my head.

Most of what I've made is gluten free with organic ingredients, per Liam's usual, but I did throw in my favorite recipe of all time.

And the oven beeps just in time...signaling my rolls are done, so I grab an oven mitt and pull them from the oven, putting them on the cooling rack.

Heaven. In. Bread.

My Nana taught me a lot of things growing up, but her homemade roll recipe is by far the best. And, just for Liam...I made them gluten free.

"Juliet?"

I look up to see Liam leaning against the doorframe, a confused look on his face. He's been out all morning running errands, so I busied myself here in the kitchen. After I made sure the house was clean.

It's been almost two weeks since the "incident", or so I was referring to it as. Things have been...weird. Liam hasn't touched me since, but whenever he's around, I still feel the same fiery tension that's always been here between us. He never brought up what happened, and so we've just been doing what we do best... avoiding each other. Pretending that he didn't have his face buried in my vagina as I screamed his name.

No big deal.

"Um, sorry if this is too much...I just...I—" I trail off, biting my lip.

Now I feel embarrassed. I shouldn't have assumed that he would be okay with this.

He steps forward, "No, don't apologize. This is very kind of you to do, Juliet. I wasn't expecting it, that's all."

"I could just tell that it's important to you. I want to help however I can."

The corner of his mouth tugs up in a rare grin, and I want to cheer. Penetrating Mr. Impenetrable. It feels entirely too good. Who knew the way inside the suit of armor was carbs.

"After all, you came to my rescue with my sprained ankle. This is the least that I can do."

His eyes lock with mine momentarily before he clears his throat and glances down at the food, then back at me.

"That was nothing. I couldn't stand to see you hurt, Juliet." His voice has dropped an octave, becoming gravelly and husky, and I clench my thighs together in response. Quite frankly, my girly parts will never be the same. Not after Liam Cartright's mouth.

Now I'm thinking about him kneeling between my legs with my clit in his mouth. Or when he speared his tongue inside of me like he wanted to eat every inch of me.

The way my name rolls off that same tongue, sweet and forbidden—

"Juliet?" he says, breaking through my daydream.

"Oh, sorry. Yeah? I spaced." I turn the oven off and start to tidy the kitchen, glancing at the girls to make sure they're okay still playing Barbies in the living room.

"Are you going to come? To the BBQ...I just didn't know if you had other plans or something."

Does this mean he wants me to be there? I never know what Liam is feeling because he's the master of holding it all inside. I wonder if he feels the same as I do about what happened? I'd never know because he's completely closed off.

"If you'd like me to be there, I can be." I quickly add, "To keep an eye on the girls so you can enjoy yourself."

"The girls will be fine. I'd like to introduce you to the team. You'll be seeing quite a bit of them when you bring the girls to games."

"Okay, yeah, I'll be there. I'll just freshen up, if you could watch the girls for just a bit?"

He nods, eyeing me as I whip off the apron and brush past him, "Of course."

At the last second, his hand comes out to stop me, grabbing my forearm lightly. The second his fingers touch my skin, it's like electricity has zapped us both.

"And, Juliet? Thank you. For everything that you do." His face is full of so much sincerity, it takes me back. For the first time, I feel like he's beginning to open up.

I'm at a loss for words, and in the moment, I just nod. The lines are blurring, and neither of us are doing very well at staying within them any longer.

* * *

I come downstairs an hour later, freshly showered, with my hair and makeup fixed, and wearing a simple dress that I picked specifically because Alex says it shows off my "banging body".

The girls have on their dresses and headbands, and they look so sweet. If there is anything I've learned in the last few weeks, it's that Liam's girls are well behaved. Sure, they have moments where they aren't. Like any children. But, for the most part, they are beyond polite and obedient. They truly make my job easy and enjoyable.

"Wow, Juliet, you look like a beautiful princess. You can be a princess with us!" "Yeah!"

Ken and Ari both rush to the stairs and slide their little hands in mine, pulling me towards the backyard. I see a few guys standing outside talking to Liam, and that means, it's showtime.

We walk outside into the backyard, and a few of the guys wave, causing Liam to look up. For the first time since I walked through his door, I can read exactly what he's feeling.

I see the flare of heat behind his eyes as they travel my body unabashedly before quickly dragging back up to my face. He likes the dress.

He walks over and bends down to talk to the girls, "Bug, Ken, why don't you guys go play on the swing set until the food's ready?"

They nod enthusiastically and sprint off to go play with the few other kids who have arrived.

When he stands, he leans in to speak, close enough that I can smell the woodsy scent of his cologne, but not close enough to touch me, "You look beautiful, Juliet."

My cheeks heat immediately, "Thank you."

He nods. Even though it looks like the last thing he'd like to do, he shoves his hands in his pockets and nods towards his players, "I'll introduce you to the guys. Their wives and girlfriends are over there." He gestures behind me to the large, round table where a handful of women sit, some rocking babies and others cooing over the babies.

Which I totally get because they are all so adorable.

Is this the life I want for myself?

For so long, Nana has been my primary focus. Making sure she was okay after Pops died. Taking care of her after she broke her hip and had to have surgery. Working doubles so much that I never had time to breathe in order to pay for her care.

It's been a long time since I've stopped and thought about what I truly want.

Do I want the family? The husband and kids? Do I still want to go to school and finish my degree?

All of these questions hit me full force as I'm surrounded by people who have their entire lives planned out and set. Lately, the same questions have begun to bubble to the surface more and more when I'm with the girls.

I'm lost in thought as I follow behind Liam, who brings me over to the group of guys he was speaking with. Each of them is so ridiculously attractive, I feel even more out of place at this BBQ. Like, seriously...it's not enough that Liam is God's gift to women, every single person he knows also looks like they walked straight off an episode of the Bachelor.

Alex would be having a field day.

I smile, thinking of my best, ridiculously man crazy best friend, and how she'd love to sink her claws, even in a nice way, into any one of these players.

"Guys, I want to introduce you to someone. This is Juliet, my... nanny." He stutters slightly, but quickly recovers, and a wide, easy smile immediately slips onto his lips.

THE NEWSPAPER NANNY

I hold my hand up in a shy wave, and each of the guys does the same.

"This is Wilson, Andrews and Williams."

The guys are easy going and completely laid back, so aside from the fact that they're professional hockey players who happen to also double as models, they make me less nervous as the conversation unfolds.

"Dinner time!" one of the wives calls from the table where she's holding a baby and a stack of plates.

I use the interruption to excuse myself and escape back into the kitchen.

Once the door is shut behind me, and everyone's conversation dies out with it, I feel like I can take a full, deep breath.

"Overwhelmed?" A voice from the side door startles me, and I nearly jump out of my skin.

It's Reed, Liam's best friend. He's leaning against the doorway, his arms folded across his chest. I can't help but notice that his muscles strain against his shirt with them crossed this way.

"Yeah," I laugh lightly, "That obvious?"

He shakes his head, "Nah, I just know what it's like to be surrounded by people you don't know. Can't remember who's who, and you're just smiling and nodding like you do."

I laugh. He's completely right. My head was starting to swim with the amount of people that I was meeting.

"You know...he's different. With you."

I stop scrubbing the counter and look up at him, "What do you mean?"

"Liam is difficult in most aspects, which I'm sure you know by now. Not an easy guy, by any means. Grumpy, uptight. You know." He laughs, shaking his head and causing his shaggy hair to fall into his eyes.

"You're good for him and the girls. They needed you, more than he probably realized. Just don't give up on him. Even when he drives you bat shit, because he will...trust me, just stick by them whenever it gets tough. They need someone to stay when it's hard."

His words pierce the already vulnerable organ in my chest that's begun to beat faster.

"I'm the nanny, Reed. Nothing more." I say, slowly. Careful with my words.

He nods. I expect him to say something in response, but he watches as I scrub the counter with more force than I intended and stands there unspeaking.

Suddenly this feels like an...intervention of some sort. It makes me wonder if Liam told Reed about our...moment in the bathroom the other night. My cheeks heat at the thought.

The last thing I want is to be shamed for coming on to my employer.

"Listen, I wasn't trying to pry or get in your business. It's just, these girls? I love them like they're my own. I've watched them grow since they were babies. Just two tiny little things. Big blue eyes that looked at me like I could hang the moon." He pauses, smiling at the memory, "It's not my place to talk about. But, you know, their mom left when Ari was just two and Ken was an infant. Liam raised them by himself. Never asked anyone for help. It's always been just him and the girls. All I'm saying is, it's hard for him to let anyone in. He's terrified of the girls being hurt. Hell, of himself being hurt, even if he'll never admit it."

"I would never hurt them."

My voice is hoarse with emotion, and I feel like I could cry, hearing Reed talk about their mother. How could their mother just leave them that way? Thinking of leaving the girls for even short term brings tears to my eyes, and I've only known them for a few short weeks. I couldn't imagine walking away and not looking back.

"Not saying you would. I just know they love hard, and the person who gets that love? They have to deserve it. He's overprotective, he and over compensates at least ninety percent of the time—we both know it. But he does it with best interests of those girls in mind. You know, he's having some problems with a guy on his team attracting bad PR. It was his idea to have the BBQ here, just so his players could feel at ease that the paparazzi won't be waiting for a shot. It's why he's so protective over the girls when it comes to the NHL life. He wanted the guys to be able to bring their families and relax, not worry about looking over their shoulders. Always putting his family and career first. Look, do me a favor and don't mention this to Liam."

I nod.

Suddenly, the back door is thrown open, and Kennedy and Ari burst through, giggling, coming to a skidding stop in front of us, breathless.

"Juliet...Juliet! Daddy said we can have cake! Actual, real cake," Ari squeals.

My eyebrows raise. Wow. Liam allowing the girls to have sugar...that's a first since I've been here. If anything, he's devout to the healthy lifestyle and makes sure that everything that comes across the threshold meets his standards. And has no qualms about letting anyone know it. Posted front and center on the fridge is a list of acceptable brands and products that he allows the girls to have, and at the bottom is a short list of "no's", with sugar being the number one culprit.

"Wow. I am surprised." I mutter.

Reed laughs and shakes his head before scooping the girls up in a fit of giggles into his arms. "Well, Juliet, I think someone very wise and wickedly handsome once told you that Liam is not the easiest person."

"Yeah, and what's that make you, then?" Liam's voice floats through the doorway as he walks into the house and looks between the four of us, shaking his head.

Caught red-handed.

"Alright, alright, enough. Everyone outside, and sugar will follow."

The girls fly back through the door with Reed on their heels, and before I can grab the pie and head outside, I look up to catch Liam's eyes on me. I feel them on my skin, caressing me.

And just as I've caught him, he's gone, leaving behind a feeling that stays the remainder of the day.

CHAPTER FOURTEEN
Juliet

The time on my Apple Watch reads eleven sixteen, and Liam is officially...plastered. Completely drunk off his ass. He's apologized no less than a hundred times, and thankfully, the girls are both asleep and tucked in tight, completely worn out from today's festivities.

"This is fucking great," Reed quips from beside me. He's been nursing the same beer for two hours, so I know he's on the sober side with me. Liam and his team member are playing a game of drunken HORSE in the backyard, and I've come to the realization that Liam definitely should stick with hockey and stay far away from basketball. I think he's only actually gotten the ball on the rim, not in, like...at all.

"Never gonna let him live this one down."

I laugh and bump his shoulder, "Let the guy relax. He's got a pretty big stick up his—". I slap my hand over my mouth.

Shit, I can't believe I almost said that out loud, and to my boss' best friend at that.

Reed throws his head back and lets out a voracious laugh, "Tell me something I don't know, Juliet. It's why he walks a bit funny, I'm telling you. Li'l cockeyed..."

My shoulders shake as I try not to laugh, but fail miserably. It feels good to talk with someone who knows Liam, and his, um... anal ways.

Just as I open my mouth to answer, there's a loud crash, and I see Liam on the ground, clutching his head.

"Oh, for fuck's sake," Reed grunts, setting his beer down.

I waste no time running over to Liam, who's sitting there, shaking his head and running his fingers through his long, disheveled hair. The same hair that I fantasize about running my own fingers through, late at night.

"Liam? What happened? Are you okay?"

The guys he was playing with are laughing so hard, they look like they're about to keel over. One guy actually does fall to the ground, clutching his stomach as he laughs.

"Fucking ball," he mutters.

"What do you mean fucking ball?"

His green eyes dart up to meet mine, and his brow furrows, "I fucking got hit with the ball, Juliet."

I pull my lip into my mouth, stifling my laugh, and sit back on my legs, "Oh."

Liam is officially the worst drunk ever.

As I think that, he sways, then falls back onto the court, grunting when the back of his head hits the concrete.

"Okay, party's over, guys," I say. I stand up, straighten my dress, then lean down and pull Liam back upright. I look over at Reed, who grins then offers a shrug and no help.

Fine.

I try to lift Liam to his feet, but if anything, it feels like gravity is bringing us both down. Finally, he gains his footing and stands, shakily.

He starts trying to walk over to his friend on the court, "Next time I'm beating your ass—"

"Alright, big guy, that's enough. Come on...let's go." I bite back a laugh as we make our way into the house. I can't believe he let loose long enough to drink, let alone actually get drunk.

"You got this?" Reed asks. We've almost made it to the door and Liam scoffs, loudly.

"I'm perfectly fine. I don't need any help." He hiccups and nearly falls over.

"Right. Juliet?"

I nod, "I'm fine, Reed. I'll just get him to bed and start cleaning up this mess."

"Nah, me and the guys can start the cleanup if you want. No big deal."

"I would seriously appreciate that. And...I might even send you home with pie."

His eyes light up, and he grins, "Say no more."

Men. So easily persuaded with food. Seriously, food is a weapon when it comes to them.

"Suck up." Liam mutters.

He's obviously not the happy, laughing drunk that I am, and it makes me giggle because the grumpy side of him is ever present, even when he's drunk.

But even drunk and grumpy, with the large stick up his butt... Liam is still amazing. He's kind and caring, and he puts his children first.

We make it inside, not very quietly, but still inside, and to the archway when Liam's foot catches the threshold and he tumbles, taking me with him. I land directly on top of him. All the hard, forbidden ridges of his body tucked tightly against mine.

He groans in pain, and I try and scramble up, seeing as how this is entirely inappropriate, since he is actually my boss, but our legs are tangled together, and with how intoxicated he is, he's not very coordinated.

"I'm so sorry," I mutter, trying to right myself.

He doesn't respond but lets out another groan.

"Juliet, uh, could you stop wiggling for a moment please," he says quietly. It takes a moment for me to realize what he means, and then I feel him. Hard, and straining against my stomach.

Oh God.

I bite my lip, "I'm sorry." My voice is hoarse and raspy, and it sounds like it doesn't belong to me.

"Nope, it's fine. All good. No problem-o."

I place my hands on the floor and lift off of him, careful not to let my dress come up, and then I reach down to help him stand. It's next to impossible not to glance down at the very large bulge in his jeans, but I do manage not to look.

Well okay, only once. Twice.

I glanced just twice, okay?

He doesn't try to stand again, simply leans against the hallway wall and rests his head.

"You know, I can't remember the last time I got drunk. Hell, it's been years. Hockey days."

I don't know what to do, so I slide down the wall across from him until I'm seated opposite.

"You have a lot on your shoulders."

He nods and swallows roughly. His Adam's apple bobs with the movement. Who knew even Adam's apples could be sexy? But somehow, Liam manages to make it so.

"Yeah. No time for getting drunk when you're raising two little girls alone."

"You're an amazing dad, and one day, they'll realize all of the sacrifices that you made to be a good father and provide a good home. Trust me."

I think of my own parents and what I would give to have even five more minutes with them. Growing up, we never had anything fancy. We were a middle-class family without many luxuries. But my father and mother had both worked hard to put a roof over our heads, clothes on our backs, and food in in our mouths. We might not have had all name brand things and trips to Disney World, but our home was full of love.

Those are the things that I remember. That my parents were hopelessly in love, and that they spent all of their time trying to convey that love to us. I remember how hard they worked, and how we would spend time together, and that I always felt happy and loved.

"My...my parents died in a car accident when I was very young. My grandmother took me in and raised me. I remember that, even though we didn't have fancy things, we had a home full of love. I was happy, and I was loved, and those are the things that

I remember. The things that matter, Liam."

He opens his eyes and looks at me, and they convey the words he isn't able to say.

"Parenting is hard. That's all I've ever wanted for the girls, you know? To be happy, and loved. To not feel any less loved since there was only me and not two parents. If anything, I've been too over protective, to make up for the fact that it's only me. That's why you're here. You know? I was faced with the choice of bringing them on the road, which makes my fucking stomach hurt, or leaving them here and ensuring that they have a normal life. Playing hockey, being a coach—it puts you front and center on every gossip site there is. I don't want them growing up that way."

My heart breaks when he says that, and I want to gather him and the girls all in my arms and hold them tight. I'm screwed.

"They are the two most loved little girls I've ever met, Liam. Both of them are angels. You are raising kind, compassionate, joyful little girls, and you're doing a wonderful job."

"Thank you. Sometimes, it doesn't feel like it. Not to get sappy on you. Too many beers." He grins.

Truth be told, I'm thankful for this moment with him. He's been so closed off and completely shut down any type of conversation with me, it's been nice to see him let me in, even if it's only because of a drunken moment.

"It's okay. I know things have been hard, and I hope that my being here has helped at least some?"

I scrunch my nose in question.

"You're a lifesaver. I know sometimes I don't...I don't act like it, but I appreciate you, Juliet, greatly. The girls love you, and I am thankful they have you in their lives. And for what it's worth...I think your pie is fucking delicious, and I hate sugar."

I throw my head back and laugh, causing him to grin in response. A genuinely happy grin that does something inside of me. Warmness blooms in my chest, all the way down to my toes.

"Well, sorry to say, I think after Reed and your friends are done, there won't be any pie left. Plus, you'll have to spend an extra hour in the gym."

"Pity. Good thing I already had two pieces when you weren't looking." He laughs.

Even though I know he's been drinking, and that's the reason for his openness tonight, I wish this moment would last longer.

That it could always be this way. But I know when he sobers up, he'll go back to shutting me out and avoiding me.

"Anyway, let's get you to bed." I stand and offer my hand to him. He slides his palm in mine and shakily gets up.

"Damn," he curses, rubbing his head. He's squinting and swaying, and I'm silently praying he doesn't fall because I'm not going to be able to hold him up. Five feet vs six foot four is not an ideal situation.

"The hallway is spinning, and there are two of you," he mutters.

"And that's our cue. Off to bed you go."

He loops his arm around my neck, and I hold onto his forearm trying to keep us both upright. Somehow, we make it to his bedroom, and when I get to the bed, he flops onto it, facedown, with an "oof."

"We should probably get your shoes off."

I wait for him to respond, but when he doesn't, I nudge him gently, and he lets out a soft snore.

Seriously?

How in the hell do men fall asleep so quickly?

Great. I reach down and gently pull off his shoes, putting them to the side. He's half hanging off the bed, and if he sleeps like this, he's for sure going to be hurting tomorrow.

Leaning across the bed, I try to push him onto the bed, but he's out. Completely dead weight.

"Liam."

My words are met with silence.

Okay, Juliet. You can do this. Just get him all the way on the bed, and he can deal with the rest. He's going to hate himself tomorrow...I just know it. I put my knee on the bed and kick off my heels, careful not to snag them on his comforter, then I start pulling him onto the bed slowly.

Jesus, how much does this guy weigh?

I'm straining and pulling, and finally, freaking finally, I get both legs onto the bed. Liam lets out a groan then grabs my waist and rolls over, tucking me against his body.

I'm so surprised I let out a squeal. His arm is wrapped tightly around my waist and my body is pressed against his while he snores lightly.

Okay, this is bad.

Really bad. What if he thinks I seduced him or something crazy like...took advantage of him? Because he's been drinking.

I groan and try to untangle myself from him, but I'm still careful not to jostle him. The last thing I need him to do is wake up and find us like this.

In my attempt to throw his heavy arm off of me, I accidentally elbow him in the stomach. I feel him still behind me and groan.

"Juliet?" he asks, confusion lacing his words.

THE NEWSPAPER NANNY

"Hi," I squeak.
"What happened?"
This night is getting better, and better.

CHAPTER FIFTEEN
Liam

I fucked up. And I realize it the moment I feel Juliet's ass wiggling against my dick.

Jesus. I almost groan out loud. I've had enough whiskey to last a damn lifetime, and my head is swimming with the amount of alcohol, but I'm fully aware of her pressed against me.

I don't remember how I found myself in this position. Honestly, everything's hazy. The last thing I remember is stumbling along the hallway with Juliet holding me up. Fuck, that's embarrassing. I should've never had those drinks with Wilson. Thank God the girls are already in bed.

Juliet immediately puts distance between us when I lift my arm off her and sit up.

"You pulled me down when I was trying to get you into the bed, and then I couldn't lift you off and—"

"Fuck, Juliet. I'm so damn sorry."

She shakes her head, "No, no. It's okay. I just…I don't—"

I don't let her finish her sentence because I pull her to me and press my lips against her soft, cherry-stained lips. Like I have been dying to since I'd had that first taste of her. For the first time in as long as I can fucking remember, I don't think. I just do the one thing I've been forcing myself not to do again after the night in the shower. I kiss her until she's breathless. Her soft, pliable body melts against mine, and I haul her closer to me, pressing my body against hers. Aligning us.

"Fuck," I mutter, pulling away from her. "I'm sorry Juli—" I start, but she cuts me off by lacing her fingers behind my neck and yanking me back towards her, sealing her lips over mine.

We're crossing a line that we can't come back from, and right now, I don't care.

I want Juliet—I want every single part of her. I want to kiss her until she's putty in my hands, then kiss every part of her body that's begging for my lips. I want to taste her again, to have her quivering against my tongue.

"Liam," she whispers, breathlessly.

She whimpers in my arms as I suck her bottom lip into my mouth and roll it between my teeth. God, I want to pepper marks all over her body. Mark her like a damn caveman.

Juliet is any man's wet dream, and she's been the star of more of mine than I'm willing to admit. I can't admit it because I'm her boss, and this...it could jeopardize everything. Briggs has already put our team in the spotlight, and it feels like every single move we make is being looked at under a microscope. Imagine if they found out about the head coach partaking in activities with his much younger nanny. How can I hold my guys accountable if I'm doing the same thing I've warned them not to do?

The question is, is it worth it? Is this tension that we've both been fighting worth risking it all?

Some things are worth the risk, and I'm starting to think that Juliet is one of those things. I'm so tired of fighting. Fighting not to catch a glimpse of her, not to inhale her sweet scent when she walks by, not to push her against the wall and leave her breathless.

"Tell me to stop," I whisper, dragging my lips down her neck, sucking, biting, and kissing until her hands yank on my hair, pulling me closer to her. Tonight, I know I can't be the strong one.

"No."

"Juliet..." I trail off, unsure of what to say. I know that I should stop this before it's too late. I should end it now and save us both the headache later, but I can't.

Now that I've had a taste, I'm addicted, and I want more. I need more. I'm fucking obsessed.

I need all of her.

"I want this. You want this. Why do we have to worry about anything else?" She pulls back to look at me. Her eyes are swimming with lust. I can see it. I can feel it in the air around us, and I'm crazy for her.

"Because it could complicate everything."

"Stop talking, Liam."

Her hands fist into my shirt and pull me back towards her. We come together in a frenzy, her hands running over my chest, my shoulders. Tentatively exploring.

I'm surprised and fucking obsessed with the fact that she's not shy and timid right now like she is whenever we're outside of this room. It's a turn on, and I can't remember the last time I've wanted a woman so badly.

She pushes me down onto my back and climbs over me, straddling me. The dress she's wearing falls onto either side of her hips, and her heat is pressed tightly against me. Her hips roll once, and I groan.

"Goddamnit, Juliet."

A grin, small and confident, graces her lips, and she dips down to kiss me once more. My tongue peeks past the seam of her lips, tangling with hers, desperate and needy.

This kiss is weeks of pent-up tension, weeks of wanting each other fiercely, despite it being wrong and forbidden. The glances we've stolen when the other wasn't looking, the times I've had to take a scalding shower and palm my dick just to keep from giving in and making her mine.

She has spent the past month driving me insane, and now I finally have her. I never want to stop touching her.

"We should stop." I say, despite the thoughts in my head.

"Stop. Thinking," she growls then grabs my hands and places them against her chest, palming her tits. I groan, my voice hoarse and rough with need, as I pinch her nipple and roll it between my fingers, inciting a breathless moan from her. I can feel how wet she is against my cock, the thin scrap of panties doing nothing to act as a barrier.

I want to rip them off with my teeth.

Juliet is a sight to be seen above me. Her cheeks are flushed, a delicious shade of pink that travels to the tip of her nose. Cherry red lips part in breathlessness as she grinds against me. Her pupils are dilated with lust, and each time she rubs herself against me, she squeezes her eyes tightly shut. I wish I could capture this moment and keep it forever because she's so goddamn beautiful it takes my breath away.

Forbidden or not, I fucking want her. I've wanted her for so long, and I am done holding back. Fuck the consequences. Fuck what everyone will say.

I wrap my arm around her waist and flip us over so she's nestled against me as I lean over her. Her legs find my waist and hook up, pressing her wetness against me once more. If I looked down, I guarantee there'd be a wet spot against my pants, which only makes me harder.

"I want to spread you out before me and drink you in. Take my time with your body. Worship every inch," I say

This moment changes everything.

There will be no coming back from this. No pretending that I haven't had my mouth on her or had her writhing beneath me. No more pretending, period.

It will never be the same.

I lift her dress, slowly, inch by inch, my eyes never leaving hers until it's bunched at her waist. Only then do I glance down and see the soft dip of her hips. She's got curves in all the places that matter. The places I'm going to spend the rest of the night worshiping with my mouth and my tongue. The tiny bright pink scrap of lace that sits in a triangle over her pussy beckons me, and just as I'm wrapping the thin waistband around my fist, the door flies open and Ari stands in the doorway. She's rubbing her eyes sleepily, clutching her stuffed unicorn.

"Daddy," she mumbles.

I scramble off Juliet and toss the blanket over her before Ari can truly see anything. She's half asleep, her eyes still closed.

"Hey bug, you okay?" I ask. I stand and quickly adjust myself before walking over to her.

She whines, "I heard something. I'm scared."

"Okay bug, Daddy is coming." Her little feet pad back down the hallway into her room.

Even though she's gone, the spell is broken and the moment is over. And now I realize how close things came this time.

"Juliet..." I start, looking back towards the bed.

"It's okay, go," she says quietly. Her clothes are tousled and she looks thoroughly kissed, and the horny part of me wants to pick right back up where we left off, but the rational part says we've made a huge mistake.

Judging by the look in her eyes, she sees my hesitation and concern. Fuck, I can't turn off my head. I can't stop thinking about all the things I could lose by doing this.

Standing here, the room still spins, and my head still swims, and as much as I wish I could pretend that the moment isn't broken, now we have to face reality.

"Go to sleep, Liam. We can talk tomorrow." She brushes past me towards the door, and I reach out and grab her arm.

"I don't regret it," I tell her.

She nods, and then, like she came...she's gone, and I'm left wondering if I just fucked up the best thing in our lives.

The next morning, I crack my eyes open with a groan. Rays of light beam into the room, so damn bright that I can hardly see, bathing me in sunlight.

Holy shit. I haven't had a hangover like this since I graduated high school. I'm too old for this shit. My head pounds, my eyes burn, and I feel like someone's taking a jackhammer to the back of my skull.

Even though I feel like ass, I remember every single detail of what happened last night, and that makes it even worse.

THE NEWSPAPER NANNY

What the fuck did I do?

Tossing back the covers, I put my feet on the ground and realize that I'm still fully clothed. I never even changed or brushed my teeth last night. Realizing that, I head straight for the bathroom and take a hot shower, brush my hair and teeth, then throw on a pair of gym shorts and a tee.

I open my door to head to the kitchen, and the first thing I hear are giggles. The kind of mischievous giggles that only mean one thing.

The girls are up to no good.

When I round the corner into the kitchen, I find Ari and Kennedy at the table with Juliet, painting on large white canvases.

Do we even have those? Juliet must have picked them up.

"Good morning," I grumble. Coffee is the only way I'm surviving today. If Reed could hear me right now, he'd call me a pussy, but I feel like I got run over by a garbage truck. I make a beeline to the coffee and pour a cup of black.

"Morning, Daddy! Did you sleep good?" Ari asks.

"I did, bug, thank you. What are you two up to?"

Kennedy holds up her paint brush to show me. She's covered in paint. There might actually be more paint on her than on the canvas in front of her. Nonetheless, she's still so cute it makes my heart hurt.

My girls. My world.

"We are painting pictures for the people at my Nana's nursing home. To brighten their day." Juliet responds. She avoids eye contact and keeps her eyes on the girls and their paintings.

Yep, I fucked this up. I need to get her alone so I can at least talk to her about last night.

"Yeah, Daddy. Look, I drew us. Me, and you, and Kennedy, and look, I added Juliet!" Ari beams, showing me the canvas before her.

"Wook, Daddy," Ken says.

I can't tell what either picture is, but they're so proud of them, my chest puffs with pride too.

Ari's brow furrows before she says, "Should I add Uncle Reed? Do ya think he would be mad if he wasn't in my drawing?"

"No, I think Uncle Reed will love any picture that you do, even if he's not in it. I think that the people at the home will love them."

Juliet smiles, but it doesn't reach her eyes. "I was planning on taking them to meet my Nana when you leave to go back on the road. She's been begging to meet the girls, and I think they would love it."

"Of course. Sounds good to me."

"Yes! I can't wait, Daddy."

"Me too!"

"That's awesome. I'm sure you girls will have a blast," I smile at the girls before turning towards Juliet. "Juliet, can I speak with you for a second?"

She looks as if she might actually say no but nods and walks into the living room without looking back.

"Be right back, girls. Keep painting your beautiful pictures."

When I walk into the living room, Juliet's sitting on the arm of the couch with her arms crossed over her chest. I can tell she's in no mood for my shit today, and I feel even worse about how things went down last night.

"Juliet, I'm sorry."

Her face hardens, and I realize she's taking my apology in the wrong context.

"Wait, I'm sorry that things happened the way that they did. Not that it happened. Listen, Juliet. Obviously, there is something between us. You felt it, I felt it, and there's no sense in denying it. But just because there is something between us, doesn't mean we should act on it."

"So, you're saying it was a mistake?" she says quietly.

"No, that's not it. No. I just don't want to risk the professional relationship that we have. You are the best thing that has happened to our family, and I truly mean it. The girls love you, and you have a way with them that even I don't. We can't lose you."

The thought of losing her sends my stomach into a twist of panic. I don't even want to entertain the thought of that happening. I can't. And I fucking hate that I put us both in a situation where it could happen. That we jeopardized her being here.

She looks down at her hands in her lap and sits quietly a moment before looking back up at me.

"You're right. So, from here on out, strictly professional."

I nod.

Even if it's the last thing I want, it's the way that it has to be. We can't be weak again.

"Strictly. There's no sense in making things uncomfortable or awkward. We're both adults. We made the decision to do this, and we can move past it."

"Almost like it never happened."

I shake my head, "I'm sorry, Juliet."

She stands from the couch and brushes past me, "Don't be sorry." When she's gone back into the kitchen with the girls, I still don't feel like I made the right choice.

Hell, I don't even know what the right choice is anymore. I'm stuck between what I want and what my family needs. At the end of the day, I have to choose what's best for the girls and for my career, no matter how badly I want to cross the line with Juliet.

I just hope that she can understand why.

CHAPTER SIXTEEN
Juliet

Liam leaves to head back on the road, and life settles down once more. I'd be lying if I said I'm not slightly sad when he leaves. Whenever he's home, the house is happier. Always buzzing with excitement, and for the first few days that he's gone, something heavy hangs over all of us.

It's even worse that he was home this time for a week. During Bye Week, there's no practice or games, so he had his first full week home in months, and the girls ate it up. They'd needed the time with him. It's an adjustment from having him home constantly, to having him on the road more than being home.

"Juliet, do you think they will want to be my friend?" Ari asks, her hand grasped tightly onto mine. I can tell she's nervous. Ken is too young to really understand, but she is bouncing around excitedly. Once we make it to the entrance, I stop walking and squat down to Ari's eye level, holding her hands in mine.

"Ari, they are going to love you. There's no reason to be nervous. My Nana and her friends are the nicest people, and they can't wait to meet you."

She nods and exhales a deep breath.

This girl is wise beyond her years, and in moments like now, she shows it.

We walk through the doors of Everwood Manor and Rachel, the daytime receptionist, greets us with a warm smile.

"Juliet! So good to see you. Who are these two cuties?" Her smile is bright and contagious. She walks around the receptionist desk to stand in front of us.

"This is Ari and Kennedy. I've been nannying for their family, and they couldn't wait to come meet Nana and everyone else."

"Well, hi girls. We are so happy to have you here. Would you like a sucker?"

Ari and Kennedy's eyes both widen. They live in a no sugar household, so when presented with the choice, they don't know what to say.

I mull over her question, but ultimately decide just one sucker won't hurt....

"One."

They jump up and down excitedly as Rachel hands them each a large lollipop.

"How about I hold these until we leave, okay?"

Ari looks at me hesitantly, like she isn't sure if she wants to give it up, for fear that she might not get it back. I almost laugh out loud when she grudgingly places it in my hand.

I put the suckers in my purse and grab each of their hands, then

THE NEWSPAPER NANNY

we thank Rachel and head towards Nana's room. I'm surprised to find that she's not in her room when we get there, and realize she must be in the main room.

Today, it's louder and more boisterous than normal, as it seems they're having a game day. I see bingo boards and the wheel of balls at the front.

Ari will love this.

Finally, I spot Nana, Gladys and Judith all sitting on the oversized sofa. Nana's knitting, as usual, Gladys is staring at Mr. Brockman with hearts in her eyes, and Judith seems to be grumbling something as usual.

We walk up, and when Nana sees us, her entire face lights up like I haven't seen in a very long time. I realize right then that I made the right choice in bringing the girls here to introduce her.

"Hi Nana. Gladys. Judith," I greet everyone. Ari tightens her grip on my hand, and Kennedy immediately lets my hand go to rush over to Nana.

"What're you doin?" she asks, standing on her tiptoes to get a better look at Nana's knitting.

It perfectly describes each of their personalities. Kennedy's outgoing and not afraid of anything, fearless in the way most three-year-olds still are. While Ari is more reserved and quiet at first, then, like a flower, she blossoms into an energetic, confident big girl.

"Hi, darling," Nana coos, "Well, I'm knitting a scarf."

"What're those?" Kennedy points to the knitting needles.

"These right here are my knitting needles."

Kennedy's eyes go wide, "I hate dem."

"No, no, Ken, these are not like the ones at the doctor's office.

These are special needles that make clothes. Like your shirt!" I tug at the bottom of her *Frozen* shirt, and she giggles. "They don't hurt, I promise. But, let's leave knitting to Nana, okay?"

I realize that she hasn't even been properly introduced and she's already opened up to Nana.

"Ari, this is my Nana. And these are her two best friends, Judith and Gladys."

Gladys smiles and gives her a wave, and Judith gives her best attempt at a smile. Perpetually grumpy, she and Liam would be two peas in a pod.

"Come see, little girl." Judith says to Ari, who looks up at me with a question in her eyes.

"It's okay, I promise. Remember, they couldn't wait to meet you. Go on."

I let go of her clammy palm and give her a gentle nudge. She walks over to Judith and stands in front of her.

"Ari, do you like bracelets?"

Ari nods more enthusiastically at the mention of her favorite thing: Jewelry.

"Well…I happen to have something special in my room that I think you'd love," Judith says. "Would you wanna see?"

"What is it?" Ari asks, fiddling with the button on her dress.

"It's a special kit that makes bracelets."

Ari gasps, "Really? Can we see?"

Now Judith has her full, undivided attention, and I'm impressed. She formed a connection with Ari seamlessly, and seems to be happier than I've ever seen her.

"Juliet, I'm gonna take Ari here to get the bracelet kit. That okay?"

THE NEWSPAPER NANNY

"Of course, Judith, that is so kind of you. We'll be right here."

Judith stands from the couch and extends her hand to Ari, who hardly pauses before sliding her hand in Judith's. Then, the two of them are off in the direction of Judith's room.

I'm shocked, to say the least. Gone is Ari's nervousness.

"Wow," Gladys mutters, "I've never seen that old fart be so nice to anyone."

"Me either," Nana quips. Kennedy has taken up a spot next to her, and is still watching intently as she weaves the knitting needle. I'm pretty sure the only times I've ever seen Kennedy so still are in her sleep and during the non-singing parts of *Frozen*.

I laugh to myself and shake my head.

This is the best decision I've made all week.

I didn't realize how badly I needed to see Nana and the girls, and the fact that they love the girls as much as I do warms my heart in ways I never imagined.

"You know, Judith doesn't have any family anymore. Just her son, who lives in some big city and pays for this place. I think he's visited once," Gladys says. Her lips are flattened in a thin, annoyed line.

Wow, I didn't know that about Judith, but then again, Judith doesn't voluntarily give information. I suddenly feel sad for her, knowing she has no family to visit her.

"That makes me sad for her."

Gladys nods. Today she's wearing a bright pink tracksuit and gold necklace, with matching bright pink feather earrings. You could, without a doubt, spot her a mile away. Typical Gladys. You can take the show girl out of Vegas, but you can never take the showgirl out of the girl.

And to think...this is a less eccentric outfit than Gladys normally wears.

"So, Juliet...tell us about how things have been going with your job?" Nana says. She peers over the rim of her glasses with a smirk. She knows exactly what she's doing.

"They're great. I love spending time with the girls, and we're still learning about each other."

"What about the hot bos—" Gladys asks, but I cut her off quickly before she says something in front of Kennedy.

My eyes dart to Kennedy, and I widen my eyes to let her know to zip it. These gossiping ladies, I swear!

"Can we just refer to him as HB, aka hockey butt."

I groan.

"Stop it, Gladys. Nana, don't egg her on!"

Nana holds up her hands up in surrender, "I didn't say anything, Juliet."

"No, but you did that thing. Where you give each other the eyes. Don't do the eyes. Work is fine. Everything is fine."

"Just...fine?"

I sigh. They're like vultures, not going to give up until I give them something.

"Yes, just fine. We're finding a good routine, and every day we fall more into a way of things. It's easier when he's home, of course because the girls miss him whenever he's gone, but we still do okay."

Ari and Judith walk back up at that moment, Ari's hands full of boxes that seem to have a billion tiny beads in them.

"Juliet, Juliet! Look! Ms. Judith gave me bracelet making kits. I'm going to make all of us friendship bracelets."

THE NEWSPAPER NANNY

"Oh my gosh, I can't wait!"

Her enthusiasm is infectious. She sits right down on the floor and arranges the boxes, then begins to go through them. Oohing and aahing over every new bead she comes to.

"Thank you, Judith. You made her entire day."

Judith tuts, "It's nothing. Least I could do. Not like they were getting used sitting on my shelf."

Judith acts tough, with an exterior made of steel, but inside, she's a big softie. And the way she's gazing at Ari lovingly as she begins to string the beads together just proves it.

"Anything exciting been happening while I've been gone this week?"

Nana, Judith, and Gladys all look at each other before looking at me. Hmm. Something happened.

"Oh, no you don't. You three aren't hiding things from me. What did I miss?"

Nana shakes her head, "Well, you know that night nurse? The cute one with the big muscles? Armando? He got caught with the other night nurse in a very..." She looks at Kennedy then back at me and puts her hand up, speaking to the side, "Compromising position, if you know what I mean."

I gasp.

"What! That's like one of your soap operas, Nana."

Gladys grins, "You know it's the most action that half of us have seen in a decade. It's all everyone's talking about."

Which explains the buzz around the building today. Who knew old people were so into gossip? Who am I kidding, they live for it. What else is there to do around this place besides play bingo and gossip about who the night nurse has gotten caught with.

"Did they get fired?"

"Not sure. They're both on leave, but I hope not because he sure was pretty to look at," Nana says.

"My daddy says that Juliet is pretty," Ari says. She's focused so intently on stringing her bracelet that she doesn't notice how I almost fall out of the chair with her revelation.

"Oh, does he?" Gladys asks smugly. The "I told you so" look written all over her face.

"Yep. I'm not supposed to listen to his phone calls, but he was distractin' me while I was trying to watch *Frozen*, and I heard him. He was talking to Uncle Reed. You are pretty, Juliet. The most pretty princess of our castle." She giggles.

Liam talked about me to Reed? Is that what prompted Reed's conversation with me during the BBQ the other night? My head swims with questions I probably won't get the answers to, and I want to groan.

I pull my phone out of my purse and check my emails and messages, then respond to a text from Liam letting him know the girls are having a great time.

He quickly replies and asks if I would send him a photo.

"Hey Nana, Judith, Gladys? Would you take a selfie with me and the girls? Liam asked if we could send a photo."

"Of course, darling, anything for HB."

I roll my eyes. "Ari, can you sit by Kennedy really quick so we can take a picture?"

She jumps up to the couch and throws her arm around Kennedy, clearly already trained when it comes to picture taking. I stand in front of the couch and take a quick selfie of all of us, and then ask everyone to make a silly face and snap that one too.

THE NEWSPAPER NANNY

I send them over to Liam and tuck my phone back into my purse.

We spend the rest of the afternoon with Nana and her friends. The girls have a blast, dancing and attempting to play bingo, but they ultimately have more fun placing all of the circles onto the page than anything. They dance, they sing, and by the time I load them into the car and buckle them into their seats, they're exhausted. I barely pull out of the parking lot and they are already asleep.

I'm glad Nana got to meet the girls today. No matter what happens with Liam, I know that the girls are a constant stream of love in my life, and I know they're here to stay.

CHAPTER SEVENTEEN
Liam

I stare at the photo on my phone for the tenth time tonight. When I asked her for a picture of the girls, I didn't know she'd send one with her in it. They have their arms wrapped around her, and all three of their smiles are enough to cause my heart to constrict.

Fuck Liam, what the hell are you doing?

Falling for a woman who is too good for me, and who doesn't deserve the shit I'm putting her through because of my own shit.

The last thing my family can handle is a scandal. New hockey coach gets caught with his nanny, who just so happens to live with us. This is exactly what Samantha warned us about. Staying on the straight and narrow, staying out of headlines, and staying off this girl, THE Puck Bunny's radar.

She has a knack for all things Avalanche, and I don't want to give her a reason to target my family.

So, despite the knot in my stomach as I stare at her, I know I'm making the right decision. The best decision for me and the girls. Not only for us, but to protect Juliet, too.

At the game tonight, the guys played like a team for the first time. Everyone worked together, and we brought home the win. I'm proud and impressed with their ability to turn it around and work as a team. Soon, they'll be unstoppable if they continue on this path. It's all I can hope for as a new coach, or hell, any coach of a team.

If we keep this up, we'll be heading to the finals in a few weeks. I can't wait to take the girls, so they can get their first real experience at a playoff game. Even if I'm nervous about having them at something as public as a game.

The flight attendant walks down the aisle a few rows ahead of me, offering refreshments and snacks, which means that we only have a short leg left of the flight. I've only been gone for three days this time, but it feels like a lifetime. Since Juliet sent me the picture, all I've been able to do is stare at it, wishing I could have been there.

Even though Juliet's Nana is obviously much older, I still see the resemblance between them. I start to think about what Juliet said earlier, about how they love to have visitors and don't get enough of them.

It gives me an idea.

We had a few days at home between games, and with THE Puck Bunny focusing on Briggs and the colossal fuck ups he seems intent on, we need some good PR. So, I call Samantha, and she says she'll work on my idea. I can't wait to run it by Juliet and see what she thinks.

Hours later, we're landing in Chicago, and I've never been so happy to be back home. We take a bus back to the arena after we get our bags, and I head straight to my SUV.

I'm determined to make it home before the girls go to bed.

THE NEWSPAPER NANNY

Glancing down at my watch, I see I have just over an hour to spare. I have one stop to make on the way home, which means I have to get my ass going.

I toss my bag in the backseat and pull out onto the highway, headed to the store that has exactly what I'm looking for. A short ten-minute drive later, I'm throwing my SUV into park and running in to snag three bouquets of the freshest flowers they have before heading home.

The clock on my dash reads eight forty-five. Fifteen minutes to spare before the girls are in bed, and my plan to surprise them is shot. I don't even bother getting my bag from the backseat. I grab the flowers, then shut the door quietly. The front door is locked, so I slide my key in the deadbolt and slip inside.

The house is dark, with no lights on in the kitchen or hallway, and the only sound is the tv playing quietly in the living room. When I walk in, I find Ari, Kennedy, and Juliet curled up on the couch, sound asleep. *Frozen* is still playing in the background.

They look so peaceful, and it kicks me straight in the gut. Juliet is a natural with them. She's attentive, compassionate, and everything these girls need. Seeing them together does something funny to my heart. I never thought I'd have feelings like this again. I never thought I'd want the things currently running through my head.

A family. With my girls and Juliet.

I swore to myself I'd never put myself or the girls in the position to be hurt again. Not after their mother.

But here I am, watching my girls sleep, and all I want is to come home to this every single night.

Their blankets lay on the couch next to them, so I gently pull them up around them, and then leave them to put up their flowers until tomorrow. I've decided not to wake them up—they seem content, and the last thing I want to do is disturb them.

Seeing the girls so attached to Juliet causes a small sliver of worry in the back of my head. What's going to happen if Juliet leaves? If she gets sick of the shit I've been putting her through? It would devastate the girls.

Fuck, I don't know what is right and wrong anymore. The only thing I know is that I'll put the girls first and do the best I can to make the right decisions. For them.

* * *

The next morning, I'm woken up by the girls bursting through the door and jumping into my bed. The perfect way to wake up.

"Daddy home!" Kennedy squeals, diving on top of me. I scoop both of them up in a giant hug and hold them to me. Just for a moment before they pull away in excitement.

"We went to visit Nana, Gladys, and Ms. Judith, Daddy. And guess what? Ms. Judith gave me stuff to make bracelets. See!" Ari thrusts her arm in my face, and I see that she has no less than five bracelets on each arm. Each one a variety of colors and different shaped beads. Kennedy then holds up hers to show the same.

"Wow, you two have been busy since I've been gone. What else did I miss?" I ask.

"Oh, nothing. I got a boyfriend at school. But Juliet says that we can't get married until I ask you first."

I choke on my own saliva when she says that. What? A boyfriend? She's five.

She's not dating until she's at least thirty-five, and honestly, even then, it will be too soon.

"Uh, bug, no boyfriends. Sorry."

"Well, that's not fair. Juliet is your girlfriend!" She crosses her arms over her chest with a "hmph".

"Juliet is your nanny, Ari, not my girlfriend."

I pull her back to me in a hug before she can protest, "Listen, bug, Daddy says no boyfriends for a long time, 'kay?"

"Okay, but can we get smoothies? It would make me happy if we could get smoothies."

"Done deal. Let Daddy shower and get dressed. Is Juliet up?"

Ari nods, "Yep."

"Okay, meet you in the living room in a few." Ari and Ken scramble from the bed and run from the room, leaving me in silence.

Boyfriends...at five years old. All I know is I am going to have my hands full with these two. I better stock up on sticks to beat the boys off with now.

I take a quick shower and get dressed, then I join the girls in the living room, where they are playing Barbies quietly.

Juliet's sitting on the couch with her legs tucked against her, watching them play.

"Good morning," she says with a small smile.

I was hoping things wouldn't become awkward between us, and I appreciate her trying to move forward.

"Mornin'."

"Sleep well?"

"Yep, what about you?"

"Good."

"I put the flowers in some water this morning. The girls loved them. Thank you."

There's nothing hidden in her tone. It's genuine. I look over at her, and she's wearing a soft smile, but still a hesitant one. She's as nervous as I am about how things will be between us. I was right when I said that everything would change after that moment, and I didn't realize how much. I hate the uneasy tension between us.

"Uh, I want to speak with you about something." She lowers her voice to a hushed whisper, "I uh, know you have a few days off before the next game, so I was wondering if I could have the night off, since you'll be home?" she asks.

"Of course, Juliet. When I'm here, you're free to come and go as you please. That's your off time."

She nods, biting her lower lip. She looks like she wants to say more but remains silent.

"Juliet has a date!" Ari squeaks.

The fuck?

Juliet's eyes go wide, and she glances at Ari, then back at me. She obviously wasn't expecting Ari to tell me. Wait, how does Ari know that Juliet has a date? Am I the only one around this house that doesn't know shit?

"A date?" I ask. My voice doesn't even sound like my own. I sound jealous, but I can't seem to give a shit enough to change it. I'm floored.

"Uh, yeah, a guy from college reached out. So, we're going to go to dinner at Antonio's tonight."

I feel like I just got punched in the stomach. Actually, I feel like I just got hit by a fucking two by four. I wasn't expecting this, and now I feel...possessive over Juliet, when I shouldn't. It's not my right. Logically, I know that, but it doesn't stop me from feeling this way. I'm the one who pushed her away, who made her feel like what happened was a mistake, even though it wasn't.

"I'm gonna go down to the gym for a bit, girls, I'll be back up in a few," I say, and leave the living room before I fuck up and do something like tell Juliet she can't go. Or say any of the shit that's going through my head right now.

I head to the basement, into the gym, and turn on the music to the hardest rock I can possibly find. I can work through this, and when I see Juliet, it'll be fine.

It's not her fault I have my own shit, and that I'm her boss. But fuck, a date?

Even thinking about her out with someone makes me insane. I head straight for the weights and pick up two fifty-pound barbells, curling them until the muscles in my arms burn and ache. It does nothing to take my mind off Juliet and her date. I wonder what kind of guy her type is? An accountant? An investment banker?

Will she wear the same dress she wore for her interview? The tight, black one that hugs all of her curves and leaves my mouth watering for a taste.

I'm going to lose my fucking mind waiting for her to come home.

But this is the way it had to be. A world where Juliet is out on dates, while I'm home with the girls. The line is clearly drawn.

I asked for this. I pushed her away, and I have no right to be mad that she's interested in someone else.

Or at least, that's what I keep telling myself as I put my body through hell to give my mind a break from obsessing over it.

It's fucked up, to feel jealous and possessive over her when I was the one who made the decision to keep things professional. Fuck, I did it because I couldn't risk losing her. Or doing anything that will put my career at risk. There were so many reasons—so much at stake.

But I still can't help that possessive feeling.

After the longest hour of my life and the most grueling work out I've ever done, my legs tremble as I climb the stairs back up to the main floor. I plan to spend the rest of the day out with the girls and not around Juliet as she gets ready for her date. The last thing I want to do is see this shit.

I hear the girls playing in their room, so I leave them to it while I take a long, hot shower and then throw on a pair of jeans and a polo. When I'm done getting ready, I find them still playing in their room. It looks like World War III has hit it, but we can worry about it later.

All that matters is being able to spend time with my girls, and making up for the time that I have to be gone.

"Hey girls, what do you say we go to the park today?"

They both look at me with excitement on their faces and a chorus of "Yes, Daddy!" rings out in the room.

I laugh, "I think we could even get smoothies? What do you think?"

"Please, Daddy!" Kennedy says, her eyes pleading.

"You got it, baby."

As we're walking out, I don't see any sign of Juliet, so I stop in the kitchen to scrawl a quick note letting her know where we've gone, and then we leave.

It feels weird to head somewhere together without her, but I keep reminding myself this is what I wanted, and this is how it has to be. The girls chatter animatedly as I buckle them into their seats and then get in the driver's seat.

"Daddy, I missed you much. I love you." Ari says from the backseat.

"Never more than me, bug."

They giggle and talk the entire ride to the park, and it just feels good. I'm grateful for the few days I have home to spend with them. For a Sunday, the park is unusually quiet. There are only a few kids sprinkled around the playground equipment.

When I get the girls out, they run full speed towards the slide as soon as their feet hit the ground. If it was up to them, they'd spend the entire day there. I sit on a bench close to the slide and watch them play.

My mind drifts back to Juliet, and I wonder what she's doing. The entire time we're at the park, I can't stop thinking of her, and the closer it gets to six, the more I realize I might have made a mistake.

By the time we've gotten smoothies and are headed home, I'm on a ledge. One that I could go over at any moment Juliet's car is still in the driveway when I pull in, but that doesn't mean anything. If her date is a gentleman, he'll pick her up.

But then again, he could be a psycho, so you know, hopefully she will be driving herself. I get us all out of the car, and the girls run inside.

"Straight to the bath, girls, you're covered in smoothie. And don't touch anything!" I yell after them, laughing when they disappear through the front door.

Walking inside, I shut the door behind me, and the first thing I see is Juliet, standing in the foyer, putting earrings in her ears.

She's wearing a red dress that puts the black dress to shame. It's flared around her hips, but still show off her curves. Tight around her chest, it shows ample cleavage. The asshole will probably stare at her chest all night, and the thought makes me feel stabby.

"Hi." She smiles and looks back at her reflection.

I really want to tell her that she looks so beautiful I want to throw her over my shoulder, carry her straight to my bed, and fuck up anyone who even looks in her direction. But, I don't. I bite my tongue, "You look beautiful. Have fun."

I don't even give her the chance to respond. Instead, I brush past her and head straight to the bathroom to bathe the girls. I'm not going to give myself a chance to fuck up and say things that I can't take back. Lately, I have a way of fucking things up without even trying.

The girls and I go through our nighttime routine, and somewhere between the bubbles and hair washing, I hear the front door slam, signaling Juliet's departure for her date.

"Girls, *Frozen* or *Moana* pajamas tonight?"

"*Frozen, Frozen, Frozen!*" they chant, while giggling.

Frozen it is. I pull their pajamas out of their drawers and grab their matching Olaf slippers. Once they're out the bath and dried off, we put on pajamas and slippers and settle onto the couch for a movie.

"Daddy, where's Juliet?" Kennedy asks. Her big blue eyes are full of questions that I truly don't want to explain to my three-year-old.

"A date, duh," Ari responds. She's brushing the hair on her Barbie doll over and over.

"Ari, how do you know so much about adult stuff?" I ask. I'm genuinely curious how my five-year-old seems to be the head of our household when it comes to gossip.

She shrugs, "I listen."

Simple.

She listens.

"Well, what else do you know about Juliet's date tonight then, bug?"

God, I'm fishing for information from my five-year-old. I need to get a fucking grip, but that ledge seems to be getting smaller and smaller by the minute.

"Hmmm. I heard her tell her friend that she needed to meet someone other than Bob. Who's Bob, Daddy?"

Jesus Christ. One, this should not be a turn on, but fuck, now I can't stop picturing Juliet with her vibrator. Worst timing.

"Ari, bug, you shouldn't eavesdrop on adults' conversations. They're meant for adults, not little girls like you. Okay?"

She looks up at me, "What does eave-s-drop mean?"

"It means that you are listening to other people's conversations when you shouldn't be. You are hearing things that maybe little girls shouldn't."

She's quiet for a moment but then she nods, "Okay, Daddy."

Now, the ledge is fucking gone. Wait…she asked for the night off. What if she doesn't come home? What if she goes to…his… place….Fuck.

There's no way she's going to sleep with this guy. That shit is not happening. I don't give a shit if I'm acting like a jealous asshole, I can't stomach the thought of him touching her.

I know I'm supposed to be strong enough to stay away, but when it comes to Juliet, I'm defenseless. Forbidden or not, I can't take it any longer. I can't pretend that I don't want her. That she isn't every fucking thing I want in a woman.

If Reed could see me now, he'd kick my ass. Truly. Tell me I've lost my goddamn mind, and to think shit through before I made a rash decision. But you know what? I've spent the past five years thinking about everything. Twice. Overanalyzing every single thing that's been thrown on my plate.

I haven't done anything without considering the girls or our future.

It's not the fucking time to think about if I'm making a mistake or not.

Before I can talk myself out of it, I make a decision. And it might be the worst decision I've made in a long time, but fuck it.

"Girls, we're going in the car for a minute, okay? Let's go."

I get up and grab them both off the couch, only stopping to grab my wallet and keys from the foyer table, and then I'm out the door.

I have one chance. I've already fucked things up, and now it's time I fix them.

The SUV is barely in park when I hop out, quickly unbuckle the girls, and walk towards the entrance.

Ari is on my left hip, and Kennedy is on my right—Olaf slippers and all—when we walk through the entrance of Antonio's. It's the type of restaurant where you wear a suit and tie, but we're walking in wearing pajamas and character slippers. I doubt they'll even give me the time of day, but I have to try.

"Hi, I'm meeting someone. Can you let me know if you've seen a woman with dark hair in a deep red dress?" I ask the hostess.

She looks at me wide-eyed for a moment before answering, "Uh, sir I'm sorry but we have a dress code, and unfortunately, we would not be able to seat you."

"I just need five minutes. That's it."

I'm two seconds from begging, but she must see the desperation in my eyes because she takes pity on me.

"Please, make it quick. I could lose my job for allowing you in."

I nod and adjust my grip on the girls.

The hostess points to the back corner of the dining room, and I can see the smallest glimpse of Juliet's hair. It's her.

We weave our way through the tables until Juliet comes into view. She hasn't seen me yet, so I take a mere second to drag my eyes over her. She looks content, but not very interested in what the guy across from her has to say.

He's average, at best. A few inches shorter than me, closely cut dark hair. His suit and tie look like they might be from Men's Warehouse. It's clear that he doesn't spend much time on his appearance, so I'm going with...accountant. Boring, but stable.

"Liam?" Juliet breathes, clearly taken by surprise at the sight of us.

I came all of this way, and I have no idea what to even say. I should've practiced, fuck recited a damn speech, before we came, but there was no time. It was now or never.

"You can't. You can't go on a date." My words come out in a rush, all running together.

Shit, I feel like an idiot. I should've thought this through more, come prepared, but all I could think about was getting here and getting to Juliet.

"What?"

Her cheeks are flushed, and they match her red lipstick.

"Look, buddy...I don't know who you are, but we're on a date, so if you could kindly leave, I'd appr—"

"Shut up."

I silence him with two words. Ari gasps on my hip, and I realize I used a no-no word.

"Daddy, we don't say that word."

"Sorry, bug."

The corners of Juliet's lips tug up into a grin, but she quickly flattens her lips and narrows her eyes at me.

"You can't come on this date because it should be me. It should be me who takes you to fancy restaurants and all the other nice places you deserve. It should be me who takes you home and loves you until the sun comes up. It should be me, Juliet. Regardless of consequences—regardless of everything."

Shock is written all over her face as I begin speaking from my heart for the first time in a very long time.

"I messed up. I should've done this sooner, and I should've pulled my head out of my as-...butt sooner, but I'm a guy. I mess up more often than not. I want you, and I don't ever want to let you go, Juliet. Give me the chance to make this right. I promise, you won't regret it."

Applause erupts around me, and I cringe slightly, not having realized how much of an audience we really have as I profess this to Juliet. The girls clap with them and dissolve into giggles.

Juliet looks around at the other people, then back at me, and shakes her head. I can see the decision behind her eyes, and I want to beg and plead right here and now for her to make the right one.

To give me the chance to show her how much she means to me and the girls.

"I'm sorry, Todd...I—I have to go." She stutters an apology, then pushes back her chair and grabs the small purse from the back of it.

"Wait, you're leaving? You're actually leaving?"

She nods, "This isn't fair to you, but some stories are already written." Her honey eyes meet mine, and it takes everything I have not to cheer in the middle of the restaurant.

"Are you comin' home, Juliet?" Ari asks.

"Yes, bug. Let's go."

Together, we walk out of the restaurant and into the parking lot. Kennedy holds Juliet's hand the entire time, and I know that this was the right choice. No matter how hard the coming days are, as long as I have Juliet and my girls, I can make it through whatever.

"You are not off the hook, Liam Cartright," She hisses once we've put the girls into their seats.

"I'm sorry, I didn't mean to put you on the spot or embarrass you...I just couldn't do it, Juliet. We were on the couch watching *Frozen*, and I couldn't stand another second of knowing you were here, with him. It made me want to punch something. I spent all day thinking about it, and by the time I heard you walk out the door, I was two seconds from dragging you back in and tying you to my bed." I pause, gauging her reaction. Judging by the way her jaw is set, she really is upset that I put this all on display for the world to see. "I'm kidding about that. I'm sorry, I really am. We need you, Juliet and not in the nanny way. You're a part of our family, and I can't do this without you. The girls need you. I need you. I'll spend however long it takes to prove that to you."

"You have lots of groveling to do."

Her eyebrows raise and she crosses her arms over her chest, which does nothing but push her tits up to the deep vee in her neckline and make me fucking crazy.

"Are you staring at my tits right now?"

I avert my eyes quickly and shake my head, "Nope, not at all. Can we talk about this when we get home? I know, big trouble."

She shakes her head again and sighs, "We'll talk about just how much trouble later. But, Liam?"

I step closer.

"Even though I'm angry...I want this, too. I've been telling myself for months that it's wrong, the way I'm feeling, but how I feel about you? It doesn't feel very wrong at all."

Instead of giving her words, I pull her to me and kiss her like I've wanted to for months. Without abandon, without worry, and with everything that I have.

Nothing, and I mean nothing, has ever felt so right. Finally, I fucking got it right.

CHAPTER EIGHTEEN
Juliet

Liam pulls the truck into the driveway and puts it in park, remaining silent. Suddenly, I'm nervous. My palms are clammy and my heart is racing wildly and unpredictably inside my chest.

I've known Liam for months. There's nothing to be nervous about, and logically, I know that. It's just that we've never been alone like this before. In uncharted waters together. As always, Liam is cool and collected, making it seem like nothing.

Me on the other hand? I bend under pressure.

"This is weird," I mutter.

He laughs, his green eyes sparkling in the setting sun behind me, "Only if you make it weird. I have no expectations, Juliet."

"Are you sure…with the girls home?" I ask.

"I'm sure. You're a part of our lives, and we're…the girls are going to know what you mean to me. I did just pour my heart out like a lovesick fool in the middle of a restaurant with them there," he says, and it alleviates some of my nerves. "But...let's just make sure they don't hear anything they shouldn't."

Okay, this is no big deal.

There's nothing to be nervous about. You're just hopefully—probably—going to have hot sex with a guy you've been wanting for what feels like forever, and after the preview the night of the BBQ, it's been torture being around Liam and not touching him.

I fumble with the door handle, then get out of the truck and get Kennedy from her seat. Liam gets Ari, and then we walk inside after he unlocks the door. Walking straight to Kennedy's room, I put her in bed, since she's already pajama clad, and she doesn't even stir.

When I walk back out to the hallway, Liam is holding Ari, who's passed out on his shoulder.

"I'm going to uh, go freshen up...while you put Ari to bed."

He laughs quietly and nods. I'm glad he's not nervous at all. Just me casually freaking the hell out. Oh God, I need to shave my legs. I should've gotten a wax, but I didn't realize that we'd have an entire night alone so soon after this monumental shift in our relationship.

Do we even have a relationship?

Juliet, stop. You're overthinking everything. Just take it how it comes. Easy.

I head to my room and quickly take a shower, shaving... everything, then washing my hair and making sure to lotion every single inch of skin.

I'm nervous, and while I'm confident about my body and who I am...Liam is a retired hockey player. He's probably been with models and actresses and other girls who put me to shame. So, I think that my nervousness is warranted.

"Let's do this. He has no expectations. Stop making it something it isn't."

Continuing to pep talk myself, I walk back out into the living room and find Liam freshly showered on the couch watching a hockey game on the tv. The girls are still asleep, which means... we're alone.

"Hi," he grins.

"Hi."

"So, I was thinking we watch a movie. One that isn't *Frozen* or *Moana*."

I laugh. What a relief, seeing as how we watch those at least fifteen times a week. I can recite every single word, probably backwards at this point.

"Only if I get to pick," I tease.

His eyebrows raise, "Oh? A guy can only handle so many chick flicks, Juliet."

"Shut up. I happen to like scary movies. Not chick flicks. You know, you shouldn't assume. What's that saying? Makes an ass out of me and y-"

He cuts me off by pulling me into his lap and pressing his mouth to mine in a kiss that speaks without words. He likes when I'm sassy, but he won't hesitate to put me back in my place.

I spent the last hour working myself up into a knot of nervousness, all for it to evaporate the second that Liam touches me. Gone. No longer even a thought. All I can think about is the feel of Liam's rough, calloused hands against the skin on my thighs.

My hands fist into his hair, tugging him closer to me as he devours me. His hands roam my body, gripping my hips, sliding up my stomach to my rib cage and palming my breasts in his hands. The groan the leaves his lips vibrates into mine, and I can practically taste how badly he wants me.

Because I want him the exact same way. A crazy, pent-up way that has been slowly eating away at the both of us for months. His tongue sweeps inside my mouth again, and I mewl against it. I should be embarrassed that I'm practically writhing in his lap, but I'm not.

I can feel how hard he is, rubbing me in the spot that aches only for him. I'd been walking around for weeks feeling a dull ache inside of me that only he can cure.

He rips his lips away from me and rasps, "Fuck, I wanted to talk before this happened."

The last thing I want to do is stop. Not when we're finally, finally alone.

The air around us crackles like live electricity, but I scramble off his lap and onto the cushion beside him.

"Can you like, not be logical for just like, a second?"

He laughs, but it too sounds as pained as I feel. I love his laugh. The way, when it's genuine, it reaches the corners of his eyes, and the skin there crinkles.

"A lot has happened in the past few days…and I just…" He pauses, closing the distance between us until my skin, still hot and splotchy from the dry humping only moments earlier, is pressed tightly against the outside of his thigh. He uses his thumb and forefinger to turn my chin to face him.

"I want to do this right, Juliet. I don't want to somehow fuck it up because I didn't take the time to appreciate what I have. I need to do this."

The sincerity in his words causes a new swirl of butterflies to unleash in my stomach. God, this man. Even when he's grumpy and uptight, he's still the kind of man who steals your heart before you even realize he's trying to.

I'm in trouble.

Serious, detrimental to my health, trouble.

My heart stands no chance when it comes to Liam. And I'm tired of fighting this.

"I want to be with you, and I want to stop being logical for one fucking second." He whispers the same words back to me, leaning closer and closer, "I just want to feel. I want this. Us. I'm done waiting, Juliet. Tell me you want this the way I do. That you feel the same as I do. That you want to make this official and not look back."

"I do, I am. I've wanted this for so long," I say breathlessly. He's so close, all I have to do is reach out and...

"There's no going back, Juliet. If we do this, then we're doing it."

I nod, "Liam, I want this."

Relief floods his face, as if he was worried I would say no. Like I haven't been dreaming of this moment, wishing and hoping that he would wake up and realize that I'm crazy about him.

"Thank God, I've been losing my damn mind."

He brings his lips back to mine and kisses me like a famished man. As if the only way he can survive is to drink me in. His hands are everywhere—my hips, my ass, sliding up my back under the thin fabric of my shirt. The feel of his hands on my bare skin sets me aflame. I'm burning for him, hotter by the second.

"I want you. I'm so tired of waiting," I pant, trying to pull his shirt over his head. He laughs when it gets stuck and he has to help me. He reaches behind his head and pulls the shirt off, tossing it aside.

I realize it's the first time I've ever touched Liam's chest without a shirt. His abs are rigid, cut and sharp. I use the opportunity to rake my nails lightly down the washboard, and he hisses in response. His abs clench and ripple against my touch, and God, my clit throbs in anticipation.

Never have I wanted anyone as much as I want Liam.

He wraps his arm around my back and stands. I let out an involuntary yelp and wrap my legs around his waist as he carries me into the hallway, but we don't even make it ten steps before his lips are on mine. His tongue slips inside my mouth, and I lose all rational thought.

He could strip me bare in this hallway, and I'd be perfectly fine with it…but, the girls are here, and Liam would probably have heart failure if they woke up.

"Shit. We need to get to the bedroom before we wake them up," he whispers quietly.

He carries us into the bedroom and shuts the door behind us with his foot, then he lays me gently onto the bed and stands before me. I can't help but admire his body. So many sharp ridges and muscles. My eyes roam over his impressive abs and wide shoulders. His body is incredible.

It makes me feel slightly more self-conscious. Not that I have much time to even consider it because he moves back over me. His hand slides under my shirt and over my ribs to my chest, and he pulls the cup of my bra. My breasts pop free. The cool air makes my nipples pebble, and Liam takes advantage of it, sucking the sensitive peak into his mouth. His mouth is warm and wet, a stark contrast to the cool air, as he takes his time showing each breast attention. His teeth leave the tiniest red marks along the swell of my breasts, marking me as his.

The possessive way he wants to claim makes me pant in anticipation. I've never seen this side of Liam. It's addictive.

"If you want to stop or slow down..." he trails off.

"I don't need either of those things." I grin, then use my leg to flip us over so I'm seated on top of him.

Without another word, he pulls my shirt over my head and reaches behind my back to unclasp my bra. My breasts tumble from the cups, and into his waiting hands.

His hands slide up my stomach to my breasts, and he palms them, rolling my nipples between this fingers and rasping, "I love your body. Everything fits perfectly in my hands."

I pull my lip between my teeth, suddenly feeling modest under his burning gaze. I look away and try to cover myself some, but he sits up and captures my wrists, "Don't ever hide from me. This body is fucking beautiful, and I want to worship every single inch."

A rush of wetness pools between my legs at his words. He knows exactly what to say to ease my nerves.

He lays me back on the plush, dark comforter, then slowly begins to work my leggings down my hips. I help him pull them off, and then they drop to the floor. One tiny scrap of lace left, and I'll be completely naked in front of him. He wastes no time wrapping the lace in his fist and tugging. The small string snaps easily, and he grins, obviously proud of himself.

"Fuck, do you know how long I've wanted to do that?" He brings the panties to his nose and inhales.

My mouth hangs open in surprise. I never expected Liam to be so...filthy in bed, but oh, am I here for it.

I sit up from my position on the bed and bring my shaking hands to his belt, slowly undoing the buckle. He looks down at me through heavily lidded eyes, and leaves me to my exploration of his body. After a few moments, I get the belt undone and pop the button of his pants. Slowly, I drag his zipper down until his tight, black boxer briefs peek through the opening. His erection is thick and rigid. The angry, purple head peeks through the waistband of his boxers, and a drop of precum beads at the head.

"Juliet..." Liam rasps.

"My turn."

I hook my thumbs in the waistband of his pants, and pull them down, along with the boxer briefs. His erection springs free, so girthy and long it makes my eyes widen slightly. If Liam notices, he says nothing, because once I get the pants and briefs down, he kicks them to the side, and I immediately wrap my fist around his cock.

The second my hand touches the velvet, silken skin of his cock, he sucks in a hiss. I look up, and our eyes lock, his full of want and desire. Pleasuring Liam is going to be almost as good as coming against his tongue, if not better. My eyes never leave his as I close my mouth over the head of his cock and lightly suck. He tastes salty and musky, exactly as how I imagined him, and it makes me hungry for more.

He throws his head back in pleasure when I take him further into my mouth and down my throat until the head of his cock nudges the back of my throat. His long, thick fingers tangle in my hair, fisting it at my nape as he guides me on his cock.

I use my hands to grasp his ass as I take him deeper down my throat until I'm almost gagging, and he groans each time he hits the back of my throat.

"Juliet, shit…I'm going to cum. Stop."

I pull his cock out of my mouth, and he reaches down and kisses me, despite the saliva and mess coating my chin.

The entire moment is so erotic that there are goosebumps on my flesh, and my nipples are pebbled so hard they hurt. As much as I love the taste of Liam and watching him as I suck him, I want him inside me. I need him.

I lay back on my elbows on the bed as he kneels in front of me, hauling my ass to the the edge of the bed, then buries his face between my legs. The moment his mouth touches my sensitive flesh, my back arches off the bed, and my hand flies to the mop of hair on his head.

"Oh God," I moan.

Liam's mouth is heaven, and I'm willing to repent for all my sins to keep it forever. His tongue flicks at my clit over and over until I feel my body tighten, ready for release, and then he stops. I look down and see a lopsided grin on his lips, "Sorry, baby, I told you I'm spending the entire night worshipping you."

He uses his middle finger to gather my wetness before he pushes it inside of me and curses when he does, "Shit, you're so damn tight." Slowly, languidly, he fucks me with his finger. Then, when the only sounds in the room are my pants and the wet slap of his hand against my skin, he adds another finger, stretching me, preparing me for his cock.

His fingers curl up and hit the spot inside of me that has me gushing around his fingers. I cry out, my release seizing my body, and my hands leave his hair and fist in the comforter. He continues to stroke inside of me, rubbing gently against me until I'm completely sated and a pile of bones.

"Fuck, I can't wait to be inside you." He climbs over me, aligning our bodies. I feel the blunt, thick head of his cock at my entrance as he hitches my leg up higher, opening me further.

"Shit, wait, a condom," he groans and drops his head to my shoulder.

"Uh, I have an IUD and haven't had sex since my last time being tested. If you..."

"My last test results with the team were clean, and I can go upstairs and grab them for you."

I stop him before he can get up, "No. No, Liam. I trust you. Inexplicably, or I wouldn't be here."

He nods, and rolls his hips against me, causing his cock to brush against my clit, teasing me. I'm already dripping, completely ready for him, and he knows it. The slickness coats his cock. He pauses, not quite pushing inside of me, to lace our fingers together, and then brings them over my head.

The same urgency is still present, but this feels...different. Liam is savoring every moment, just the way I am.

When you wait for something for so long, it makes it that much better when you finally have it. It's beyond worth the wait.

He presses forward, inch by inch, sliding inside of me. He's so big, and thick, and I feel so... full. His movements are controlled, and tender. Unlacing our hands, I run mine down his back, scoring my nails along the skin as I go.

"Liam," a breathy moan escapes my lips.

Once he's fully seated inside of me, he pulls out and thrusts back in slowly, again, and again until I'm writhing in agony. I need more.

"More," I beg.

His eyes turn molten, and he grabs my foot and places it on his shoulder then thrusts deep. So deep that when he swivels his hips to hit the secret spot inside of me that, until today, only I've been able to reach, he brushes against my clit and it pushes me closer to the edge.

Leaning down, he captures my lips while he fucks me. His thrusts become harder, faster, deeper. Then, he pulls out and flips me over to my stomach.

"Is this okay?" He grunts.

"Yes!" I practically sob.

I'm so desperate for release and wound so tight, I'm going to fall the moment he touches me. He puts me on my hands and knees in front of him, then grabs my hips and pulls my ass up to him. He gathers handfuls of my ass and pulls me towards him. I can feel the head of his cock against my entrance, and he slams back inside of me in one swift motion.

I cry out in pleasure as he bottoms out inside of me. He pulls out slowly, then slams in again, fucking me so hard I slide up on the bed with every thrust. He's so deep inside of me he feels like he's inside of my stomach, and I've never felt like this.

So completely wild and crazed. I've always been a shy, quiet lover. But Liam is bringing out a side of me I've never met. Apparently, I've never been thoroughly fucked until tonight.

When he brings his thumb to my clit and circles it, I can feel the orgasm begin. Combined with his harsh grunts, and the erotic sound of his balls slapping against my skin with his brutal thrusts, I explode around him.

My back arches, and I fall face first into the bed as I experience the most powerful orgasm of my life. It seizes my entire body, and pleasure blooms inside of me, flourishing until it's taken me over wholly. I barely recognize the throaty moans that leave my lips, hardly even notice Liam groaning behind me, gripping my hips as he stills and spills inside of me. I feel the warm ropes of cum coat my insides as he thrusts even deeper inside of me. A second orgasm takes me by surprise, and I push back against Liam. He groans as his thrusts slow.

I'm not sure what just happened, but what I do know is it's the best sex I've ever experienced. The most intimate. Two orgasms? Back-to-back?

"Holy. Shit," Liam says as he gently pulls out of my body. I collapse onto the bed and cuddle into the comforter, completely dead and out of energy to move.

"Yeah." I giggle.

"You're incredible, Juliet," he says, dropping a kiss to my lips before leaving the bed and going to the bathroom. I hear the faucet run, and he comes back with a warm rag to clean me up. Also...a first.

It just goes to show how attentive and caring Liam is.

Right now, I'm in an orgasm coma, but later...When I'm back in my right mind, I'll obsess over the fact that this just happened, but for now, I'm going to remain in my bliss. The bed dips, and Liam comes up behind me and pulls me into his body. He holds me tenderly and trails kisses against my shoulders and back.

Who knows what tomorrow will bring? But, for the first time in a long time, I'm happy.

CHAPTER NINETEEN
Juliet

"Wait...you did what?" I screech.

Liam gives me a smile that makes the fickle heart inside my chest beat faster, so rapidly that it might give out if he keeps it up. He's too handsome for his own good. Which is why he just dropped this news on me like a bomb, and I'm not exactly sure how to feel about it.

He shrugs, "The guys are going to go to the nursing home that your Nana's at and pose for a calendar."

I shake my head, squinting my eyes and trying to figure out what exactly is going on, "Wait, wait, wait. How did this happen? Like...whose idea was it?"

"Mine. Well, mine and Samantha's. She's in charge of PR for the team. One of my players is having a rough go, getting himself into trouble. In an effort to clean his image and boost ours, we need some good PR. So, after talking to the girls, and seeing how much fun they had and how happy they were just from visiting...I thought, what better of an opportunity? Not to mention, all proceeds of the calendar sale will go directly to the nursing home."

Wow. I know how much they could use the money, and if it helps Liam out, then honestly, I'm all for it. I'm just taken back that all of this went on and I had no idea. Liam seemed to orchestrate it all behind the scenes.

"That's very kind of you to put together. They could use the money."

He nods, and gives me another show stopping smile. One that he's been sporting the last two days since the restaurant, and us officially becoming a couple.

Although things have changed between us, and there are lots of stolen kisses and hidden touches, we haven't really been able to explore what it means to truly be crossing this line into new territory. Becoming a couple. After all, Liam is a full-time single parent, and we are both too afraid of the girls busting in or catching us in a compromising position. Neither of us is ready for the conversation that would ensue from that.

"When is this happening?"

He glances down at his watch, "In the next two hours. Which means that we need to be getting ready and heading that way."

Wait...if Liam's entire team is going to be at Nana's nursing home...that means Liam will be meeting Nana. And Gladys. And Judith.

I groan, "I'm not sure if you can handle Nana and her besties."

He laughs out loud, throwing his head back and letting out a loud rumble, "You act like I don't have a team full of guys who are permanently stuck in their teenage years. I can handle your Nana, babe."

The name causes a swirl of butterflies to erupt in my stomach. This is so new, so different from what we've been doing, I'm still trying to get used to being...more to Liam.

Starting with pet names like babe.

"Later, I'm telling you 'I told you so'."

Walking into Everwood is like walking onto the set of a photoshoot. There are oiled up guys with ridiculous props, large backdrops, even larger cameras, and a gaggle of old women standing by the side, practically in heart failure.

Remind me to kill Liam later.

Speaking of which.. where is he?

I look around the building but see no sign of him. What I do see is Nana, Judith and Gladys standing next to a shirtless guy with enough oil on him that if he stands next to a fire...he's going up.

What in the world is happening? When Liam said they'd be shooting a calendar, I didn't realize that he meant "Hockey Players Gone Wild: Nursing Home Edition."

Nana gazes up at the guy lovingly. He offers her his arm, and she squeezes it then giggles.

My God. I can't take it.

I'm thankful the girls aren't here to witness it. No wonder Liam called his sister and asked for an impromptu sleepover. He knew this is what we would be walking in to, and I can't imagine having to explain that to Ari, who has fifty questions a minute.

I walk over to Nana and her posse with their model and interrupt by pulling her away, "Nana, what the heck is going on?"

Gladys giggles loudly, "Oh, Juliet, your Liam orchestrated all of this. We're going to be participating in the shoot! Can you believe it? Well, only those who would like to, but you know we couldn't pass it up."

"Uh huh, is everyone clothed from the waist down?" I ask, but I'm genuinely afraid of the answer.

Nana tuts, "Oh, Juliet stop it, everyone's got their pants on... for now."

That's it, I've got to find Liam before I see something that I can't unsee.

"Okay, I'm going to find Liam so I can introduce you. Please, keep your hands to yourself, ladies. Seriously." I say it directly to Gladys because she's the one most likely to snag a hockey player and ride off into the sunset, or so she would think.

I leave those three standing with the players and walk through the building looking for Liam. I finally spot him in an intense conversation with a woman who looks like she might be a lawyer. I hesitate to approach, not wanting to interrupt their conversation, but Liam waves me over.

"Hi," the girl with the stern face and fierce business attire says. "You must be Juliet?"

I nod and hold out my hand, "Yes. Hi."

"I'm Samantha. I work with the team and manage their PR and events. What a success this is, right?" She grins.

Yes...just very unexpected.

She must read the look on my face because she laughs, "Not what you expected? Me either. But the guys brainstormed this when we brought the idea to them, and we said why not. We've already had a ton of preorders, so it seems like we'll be able to donate a good amount of money to Everwood."

"Yeah, they could really use the money to update their buildings and buy things they've been putting off. My Nana loves it here. The staff is so kind and friendly, and they truly put their patients first."

Samantha looks around at the packed main room and smiles.

"It's an honor to be here. I'd love to meet your Nana, Juliet, have you seen her?"

I nod, "Uh, well, last time I checked, she, Judith and Gladys were pretty hands on with one of your players. I told them to keep their hands to themselves, but trust me—don't leave those three unattended."

Liam laughs, and we say our goodbyes to Samantha before heading back towards the front, where Nana and her girls are.

"You know, it's honestly so fucking nice to have a day where we're not the black sheep of Chicago in the media. A whole day of no negative PR. Only good shit. We need more days like this."

"Don't get ahead of yourself just yet...I feel like I should warn you again. Nana and her friends are what most people would call a hot mess."

"Are you embarrassed to introduce me to your Nana, Juliet?" Liam teases. "Want to keep me a secret for longer?"

"Oh, you're definitely not a secret. These three have been not so secretly rooting for us from the start. Trust me, every time I'm here, I hear about it."

We approach Nana, Judith and Gladys, who are still standing to the side of the backdrop, watching as the photographer takes shot after shot of the shirtless guy. They must be sixty years his senior, but the way he keeps shooting winks their way, they couldn't care in the least.

"Nana?" I say.

She looks over and her entire face lights up when she sees Liam. It causes warmth to spread in my chest. She looks so happy to see him.

"Oh, you must be Liam," she coos. Instead of offering him her hand, she pulls him to her in a hug. He never hesitates before wrapping his large arms around her small frame. He completely swallows her. She sighs happily before pulling back to get a better look at him. "You know, you're even more handsome than she said you were."

Oh God.

I laugh nervously, "Ha-ha, Nana, let's not talk about the things I've told you, okay?" I turn towards Gladys, "Gladys, Judith. This is Liam...my..." I trail off.

Hell, what do I call him?

"Her boyfriend, and her boss, but we're not big on titles," he shrugs and answers for me. The wide grin on his face shows just how done he is with labels, and lines, and I want to kiss him right in the middle of this nursing home.

"It's a pleasure to meet you, Liam. We've heard so much about you. Oh, and you just have the most darling little girls. They were so sweet, and their manners...let me tell you, I haven't met children in a very long time that had manners like your girls did."

"Thank you, Gladys. I work very hard to teach them to be respectful and always use their manners."

Her face softens even more. She's all but a puddle at his feet. It's like...I don't understand. The man is the most charming, ridiculously and effortlessly handsome grump I've ever met.

"So, I hear you put all of this together," Judith waves towards the photographer.

"Yes ma'am, I did. We needed some team events, and the girls told me how much they enjoyed their visit, so I figured, what better way to give back to the community. Now, the calendars...I can't take much credit for. That was all the guys. They are a creative bunch, when it comes down to it."

"Oh, I see it." Judith mutters.

Liam grins at her response. I was worried Nana and her bunch would be too much for Liam, but he seems to take everything they say in stride.

Hours later, after Nana, Gladys, and Judith have taken enough photos to fill three calendars, and Liam hopped in for a shirtless picture that has my mouth watering and my thighs clenching in anticipation, it's time to leave.

He makes his way around to Nana, Judith, and Gladys, giving them hugs and a peck on the cheek before coming back to stand by me.

"Ladies, this was the best day I've had in a long time. Thank you for all of the laughs. I can't wait to come back. My schedule is a little crazy right now, but when it's off season, you bet I'll come visit as much as I can."

All three of them basically swoon and melt into a puddle at his feet.

"Liam, we truly enjoyed it. We are truly so thankful for you putting all of this together."

"It's my pleasure, really."

I make sure to give Nana an extra squeeze before I leave

because heaven knows she's crazy, but she's mine. She's been the best Nana I could have ever asked for, and she's sacrificed so much for me. If she wants to spend her golden years rubbing down hot, oily, hockey players...well then, I guess I better just deal with it.

"Behave, ladies. I'll come by soon, hopefully with the girls. Judith, Ari can't wait to make more bracelets with you. She's been talking about it nonstop."

Judith smiles, then flattens her lips back into a thin, annoyed line.

Yeah, I see you, lady. Act as hard as you want—that little girl owns your heart, just like she owns mine.

That's the terrifying part of things changing with Liam. No matter what happens, the one thing I can't stand to lose are those girls. They're my heart, and I never break pinky promises. I'm not going anywhere.

CHAPTER TWENTY
Liam

There are very few moments in life that you remember vividly, no matter how many years have passed. Moments that are so impactful, they change your life and alter the future. Ones that, even twenty years from now, you'll look back and remember like they were yesterday. The feeling, who surrounded you, the smell, the taste, the look.

I'm living one of those moments right now, and I can honestly say that, no matter how much time passes, I will never forget the way it feels. Standing in the middle of the ice with my team, my found family...celebrating a playoff win that puts us at the Stanley Cup.

These guys have worked their asses off. Put in time, blood, sweat, tears. Made sacrifices. Trained harder. Missed their families. Put their bodies through hell. They did all of that because, like me, they live and breathe hockey. As an athlete, you condition yourself to a lot of things. Physically and mentally. And these guys did it all, without complaint, and I couldn't be fucking happier to call them my players.

That's all I've wanted in this career. To be the coach of a team I'm proud of. And not only did we win, we won by a damn landslide.

I'll never forget the crowd chanting our name. It echoes and bounces off the walls of the arena. Thirty-five thousand people. It feels unbelievable. Surreal.

The only thing that makes it better? Knowing my girls are in the crowd right now. All three of them. I get to walk off this ice and hold them in my arms while we celebrate this life changing moment in my career. While I'm standing here, soaking it all in, the guys soak me... literally.

An entire jug of Gatorade poured over my head, soaking me from head to toe. Fuck, that's cold.

"We fucking did it," Reed yells in my ear so close it rings, but I slap his back and holler with him. We all do. This is our fucking moment.

Soon, we're ushered off the ice into a crowd of family and friends, and straight ahead, I see my girls. Ari's on her tippy toes, barely able to contain her excitement, and Kennedy is holding onto her hand smiling from ear to ear. What's even better?

Juliet is standing beside the girls, and she's so fucking beautiful it takes my breath away.

I walk over to them and bend down, pulling both girls into my arms for a tight hug.

They squeal whenever I tickle them, "Hi bug. Hi baby."

"Daddy, you won!" Ari squeals excitedly.

I nod, "We did, bug. Can you believe it?"

"Course I can, Daddy. You're the knight, remember? You always save the day!"

Juliet laughs, soft and sweet, and I want to bottle it up and keep it to myself. "I think this is definitely cause for celebration."

"Hmm, what do you girls think?"

They look at each other, then back at us, then Kennedy says, "McDonalds!"

"You've never eaten at McDonalds in your life. Why in the world would you choose that, Ken?"

She fidgets with her hands before shrugging, "I saw on tv."

I guess there are worse things in life than McDonalds, even if there is an ass load of grease...and carbs. You know, there is a reason my kids don't eat overly processed shit like that, but if that's where they want to celebrate, then so be it.

"Let's do it."

And that's how I find myself sitting in the McDonalds parking lot eating cheeseburgers and greasy french fries.

I can't remember the last time I threw caution to the wind, ate shit that's so bad for me I'm sure I'll regret it later, and laughed until my stomach hurts. But this dinner date celebration is exactly what I need.

"I can't believe you don't eat McDonalds french fries," Juliet moans around a mouthful of fries, and it causes my dick to stir in my pants. Pathetic, I know, but I can't help it. I'm crazy over her. I want my hands on her any and every chance I can. And...when she moans like that, my mind immediately flashes back to a few days ago when I had her spread out on the bed and my mouth on her pu—

"Liam?"

Her voice pulls me from my thoughts. I didn't even realize I had zoned out of the conversation. Another reason she's so dangerous for me.

"Sorry, what?" I ask, taking another bite of my burger.

"I said, tomorrow there's a fair downtown. I wanted to take the girls." Her eyes shine with excitement.

Kennedy gasps, and immediately says, "Please, Daddy."

"Sounds good to me. I have some work calls in the morning, but I'm free for the rest of the afternoon."

Juliet smiles, a secret smile, and I wish I could lean over and kiss her. We decided that we won't make our relationship known without trying to explain it to the girls, and we're taking it slow. Enjoying the quiet, without the outside world looking in.

Once we finish our food, we throw everything away and head home. Even though we're not far, the girls fall asleep in their car seats before we even hit the interstate. They've had a long, exhausting day, with a lot of activity they aren't used to. Being in an arena packed with thirty-five thousand people gives you an adrenaline rush, no matter where you sit. The buzz of a crowd, the winning buzzer sounding, and the entire arena exploding on a roar. Hell, I usually crash after a game and sleep twelve hours.

I pull my SUV into the driveway and shut off the ignition, then I look at Juliet. She looks back at the girls and laughs, "Those girls are exhausted."

"That just means the shower I've been waiting all night for can include you." I grin.

I see the flare in her eyes at my suggestion, and fuck, I can't wait to strip her bare and have her to myself for the entire night. We each get one of the girls out from their car seats, and after I unlock the door and disarm the alarm, we carry them straight to bed. I don't even bother with bath time, since they're both out like a light. Just tuck them in and turn on their nightlights.

Just as I shut off the light in Kennedy's room, I feel my phone vibrate in my pocket.

I pull it out and answer, "Cartright."

"Liam, have you been online?" Samantha's voice comes out in a rushed panic. I've never heard her this way, and it immediately causes me to stop in my tracks. Something's wrong.

"No, I just got home and got the girls in the bed. Is it Briggs? Shit," I curse.

She exhales, "No, it's worse. Check your email. Now."

Kennedy's door clicks as I shut it behind me quietly, and then I take the stairs two at a time, heading straight for my office to pull my email up. When I get it up and open it to the most recent email, after a slew of unread emails from everyone I know, I get a feeling at the pit of my stomach. A sense of dread.

Something bad has happened, and I'm not going to like whatever I'm about to see from the sound of it.

I click the open button, then click the link that she's sent, and the first thing that pops up is a headline that reads, "NHL hotshot coach seduces younger live-in nanny". When I scroll down, there's a photo of me and Juliet, my hands laced in her hair and her hands fisted in my shirt from the kiss at Antonio's.

Who the fuck took this photo? Someone was watching us, and I had no absolutely no idea who.

From the angle, it looks like I'm devouring her and she's hanging on for dear life. You couldn't have caught us in a more compromising position if you tried, unless you'd peeked into the bedroom the night the girls went to Shana's. My chest begins to tighten as the anger seeps into my veins.

I'm pissed. Not only has mine and the girls' privacy been invaded...so has Juliet's.

Goddamnit. This isn't just bad, this is worse. The fucking worst of the worst. How did they even get this picture? It was nearly dark, and it's not like we were standing in the middle of a public space. We'd been in the back corner of a parking lot, completely out of view. Worst of all...had they been following us to capture this? Were the girls going to be thrown into this shitstorm?

So many questions fly through my head, I can hardly keep my cool.

"Fucking media. Damnit!" I hiss.

"Liam...there's more. There are photos of the girls, keep scrolling."

My heart stops in my goddamn chest. This is my actual worst nightmare. The girls... being exploited by the damn media for a headline.

The photos are of the girls in their pajamas as I carry them to the car, and as I buckle them in.

"I want this shit taken down. Now. These are my fucking kids, Samantha. They're children." I flex my hands after I realize that I'm making fists so tight my knuckles are turning white. I tried to protect them, and I failed.

And now their photos are all over the goddamn internet, and there's nothing I can do to stop it. A wildfire burning out of control. A wildfire I started, even though I would never do anything to hurt my girls. They're my life.

"I know. We're already on top of it, trying to have it taken down from the site and doing damage control. But Liam, you should've told me this. We could've prepared, or at least not been blindsided by it. We discussed this. We said no headlines, nothing to draw negative attention to the team. And you sure did get a headline. Big and bold. Damnit, Liam. Tell me what the hell is going on."

She's pissed that I didn't tell her this beforehand, but this…this is what I was trying to protect both Juliet and my girls from. The invasion of our personal, private lives.

I drop my head into my hands and let out a defeated sigh. What can I even say? I'd known this was a possibility, and I'd done it anyway. I knew what a risk I would be taking by getting involved with Juliet, knowing she's my employee. Our nanny. How the world would view it.

And now the consequences are about to bite me in the ass, royally.

"We're together. I didn't bring it to you because I don't like to share details of my private life, Sam. I'm a private guy, always have been. Especially when it involves my family. Not to mention, it's new, and I don't have to report when I date someone."

"Well, the world knows now. I just wish you would've told me."

I exhale, the tightness in my chest constricting by the second. I can't believe this is happening. The headline…the photos…the fact that now my girls are on a damn gossip site like they aren't just little girls. All of it makes me fucking terrified, "Does Mark know?"

She sighs, "Yeah. He's pissed Liam. We discussed this. Stay out of headlines. Good PR only. He saw a headline that said "Stanley Cup win tarnished by NHL Nanny Scandal" and I thought he was going to have a coronary. I've discussed it with him and the team, and we need to get in front of this before it escalates any further. We have to get in front of it before your career is unsalvageable. We're going to have to schedule a press conference, and you're going to have to speak, Liam. Clear your image."

Ice floods my veins. God, what am I going to do if I lose my coaching position? Not just me...but the girls. I could lose the house. Have to move them from their school. The house they've grown up in since they were babies.

"Samantha, you know how much I hate to have my private life on display. A fucking speech? About my relationship? About my family? Hell no. I refuse to sacrifice our privacy just because a tabloid is exploiting us. It's bad enough these assholes have photos of my girls attached to these damn ridiculous headlines."

"It's not an option. At this point we're purely doing damage control, and a new NHL coach sleeping with his recently employed nanny screams scandal, and you knew this. The public will view it as you taking advantage of a younger girl by using your power of authority."

My stomach clenches at her words. Fuck, I'd never do anything to hurt Juliet or take advantage of her, but it doesn't matter. People will view things how they want to. Perceive our relationship in a negative light. And there's nothing I can do about it but get in front of a goddamn podium and pretend I'm okay with putting my private life, my private relationships, on display.

But what else can I do in this position? My reputation as a coach is now tainted by this, even though we've done nothing wrong. The world isn't looking at it this way. If this is the only way I can salvage my career and make sure my girls are protected and out of the media, then so be it. The less attention on us, the better. If I do this, it'll blow over...I hope.

I rub my temples, trying to rid myself of the headache that has suddenly taken over.

"Fine. Whatever needs to be done. In the meantime? What do I do? Can we get with Chicago PD and have someone in front of the house? Briggs had people outside of his house after the last headline, and I don't want that here. My girls' safety is my priority, always."

Every second of this conversation causes my gut to twist more and more with helplessness and rage. I want to put my fist through the wall, and I'm not even a violent guy.

"Of course. I'll get online with the captain and see what we can arrange. In the meantime…we schedule the press conference and let the waters cool. Give it time to blow over. Let's try and save your career. You know as well as I do, you could have reporters camped outside your house looking for a glimpse of the two of you together, Liam. Taking the trash out... walking to the car. You know that they have no qualms about invading personal space."

"Who originally posted this?" I squint, looking closer at the email, and then I see. "THE Puck Bunny. Go fucking figure. Why is this damn girl so damn determined to fuck with my players and my team?"

Jesus, my guys.

They've worked so damn hard all year for this, and now their win is tainted by this fucking headline, and this damn blog who can't seem to move on to something bigger and better. I feel so guilty right now.

"I have no idea. We haven't been able to find any information. She's like a ghost. Either she's super good at tech and hiding all traces, or she has someone doing it for her. All I know is that picture is all over every gossip and sports site in the country. We've got to get ahead of this."

I don't know how to fix the situation that we're in. I feel guilt for bringing Juliet into our lives, and now she's being dragged through a media nightmare. But her being here...it's a beacon for reporters and paparazzi. It puts the girls at risk.

"Should...should I let her go?"

Even saying it out loud feels like something bitter against my tongue. It's the last thing I would ever want to do. Fuck, we just decided to be together. To take the plunge of a new relationship, and now I feel like I'm having to choose between her or my girls. Their safety. Their daily lives are at risk. Normalcy as they know it will be out the window with these reporters outside the house.

The police.

They won't even be able to go to dance class without having a traill of people at the door, cameras in their faces as they come out.

"I think that, if you terminate her, it's going to look even worse if the media finds out. I think right now, it might be best to put some space between you and Juliet until this dies down. Just for a few months, until the media latches on to something else and you're old news. Until we can do damage control and see if we can save your job."

Space. I wanted anything but space from Juliet.

The words echo in my head causing the knot in my stomach to tighten. Like it's so fucking easy. To just somehow remove Juliet from our lives, like she isn't the tape that has held us all together for the past few months. My girls love Juliet in ways that I can't even begin to understand. They are comfortable, they have a routine.

I have no clue how I'm going to do this. But the ultimatum has been given. The line we have crossed clearly before is now being drawn again.

Juliet...or my career.

An impossible choice, but one I'm forced to make.

No matter what I choose...mine and the girls' lives will change forever.

CHAPTER TWENTY ONE
Juliet

The celebration high we have been riding for the entire night fades the second Liam walks into the living room. His face is murderous. The anger practically radiates from him, and I'm immediately on alert.

"What's wrong? Are the girls okay?" I hop off the couch towards him, and he shakes his head slightly.

"Juliet, we need to talk."

He sounds pained, completely out of sorts. Nothing like Liam, and it sends panic through my body in a wave. What could have happened in the short time he was upstairs?

"Tell me. What's happening?

I sit back down on the couch, but this time I'm anxious, and I can't stop fidgeting. Another trait carried over from childhood.

"You're scaring me, Liam. What's going on?"

"The last few months we've been...targeted for the lack of a better word. By a gossip site that has some kind of…I don't know… vendetta against Briggs, my player. He's found himself in trouble, and I've been working with Samantha and the team owner, Mark, for the past few months. Trying to get us any good PR we can find. Volunteering at the soup kitchens, donating to charity, visiting the children's hospital. Except today…all of that went to shit, and it's my fault."

He sits down next to me on the couch, and I want to reach out and rub the worry lines from the corner of his eyes. Whatever is going on is bad enough to have his usually calm and collected demeanor completely disarrayed.

"THE Puck Bunny, the gossip site, somehow got a photo of us in the parking lot at Antonio's kissing, and it's everywhere, Juliet. Headlines are saying I seduced my younger nanny, and that the Stanley Cup win is tarnished from the scandal. It's horrible. I'm worried sick about the girls. The media is relentless. They don't stop until they have the story, or they have something. They'll dig further into our lives, and I can't let all of this happen to my girls."

I swallow thickly, "Of course, they're your girls, Liam."

"This is bad, Juliet. Not just bad, it's a fucking nightmare. My entire career is in jeopardy. I could lose everything. I mean…The girls…I—" He stands abruptly, dragging a hand down his face in frustration. I can feel the anxious panic radiating off of him as he begins to pace the space in front of us, "I knew it was a possibility when we got involved, we both did. I just didn't think it would blow up like this. I didn't imagine that our lives would be impacted this way. It's blown up in my face in a way I never imagined and left me with impossible decisions."

I hear everything that he's saying, but his words don't truly sink in until he speaks again, and only then do the words pierce my heart.

"Juliet, we have to end this."

I swallow thickly, my pounding heart plummeting to my stomach, "What?" My voice is a hoarse whisper. How can he say that? No matter what is being thrown our way. I stand from the couch in earnest, but don't make a move to go closer. I don't know if I can. My heart is pounding so hard in my chest I might fall over from the force.

"I'm sorry. The girls, Juliet. I'm doing this for them. I have to protect them, at all costs, no matter what it takes. I just think right now, with the media and the headlines, it's better if we take time apart. At least until this blows over. Until we don't have to worry about damn reporters camping outside of the house to get a photo of us."

"So not only are you breaking up with me, you're also taking the girls from me."

Even though I try to tamp them down, tears well in my eyes. This hurts more than I ever expected it to. Not that I ever expected to be in this position, regardless of whether I knew it was a risk we were taking from the beginning.

He opens his mouth to speak, then closes it like my question surprised him. Whether he realizes it or not, I love those girls more than anything, and I will always want to protect them and shelter them from the cruelty of this world.

"I'm sorry, Juliet. I'm sorry. I think right now this is the best decision. Fuck, do you think this is what I want? The last thing I want is to hurt you, or to pull you into this. I feel guilty enough that you're a part of this. I'm sorry for all of it. Samantha is doing everything she can to have the photo removed and get headlines under control, but she said it's spreading like wildfire. Soon, they'll know your name and address, and I just can't risk my career or my girls any more than I already have."

"So, what you're saying is that your career is more important than what we have?"

"No. No, that's not what I'm saying. What I'm saying is that, right now, I have to make a decision between my family and my career, and our relationship. It's not ever a decision I thought I'd be faced with, but I had to choose."

My heart seems to shatter into a million tiny shards on the floor in front of him. A second longer, and I fear I may fall apart with it. Never in my life have I experienced such hurt, anger, and betrayal.

His eyes swirl with hurt and more emotion than I've ever seen, and I wish I could go to him and comfort him, even though he's the one hurting me. This is all too much. How can he discard me so easily? Like what we have means nothing?

He steps toward me, and I take a giant step back, creating space between us and holding up my hand to stop his prowl forward.

"Juliet, please. Don't be like this. I'm doing what I think is best. The situation is impossible. No matter what choice I make, someone gets hurt. I think it's best if we end this now so, in the end, the girls don't get any more attached, and it can be a clean break."

"You know, Liam, since I've met you, I have admired and respected everything you do for your family. I love those girls with all of my heart. I've fallen for them just as hard as I've fallen for you." His face morphs into a mask of pain at my admission. I hope it hurts as much as he's hurting me. I hope my words pierce him the same. "I just thought that somewhere along the way, after everything, you felt the same way about me. That I was a part of your heart, just as much as those girls. I would never, ever want you to have to choose between us. I would choose them every time. I just didn't take you for the kind of man who runs when things get hard or takes the easy way out. You didn't even fight for me. You didn't take time to process what was happening. A knee jerk reaction, and now I see very clearly everything that I should."

"That's not what's happening here, Juliet. I'm not saying that this is forever. I just need to put space between us while this all is going on."

I laugh, the sound hollow and humorless, "You made your decision, Liam, and I hope that you're able to live with it. Please tell the girls that I love them, and to make sure to brush their teeth when they wake up."

With that, I don't wait for his response. I leave him standing in the living room while I go pick up the pieces of my fragmented heart. Of all the times in my life I have had to be brave, this isn't one of them. I don't look back.

Somehow, I manage to drive to Alex's house and get there all in one piece. Well, except for a broken heart. I'm not even sure where the pieces are scattered anymore.

She waits for me at the door with wine, ice cream, and nineties movies ready. The cure for any broken heart, or so I thought. Because it doesn't seem to help in the slightest. I miss the girls fiercely, and it feels strange to be separated from them, even if only for a night.

I can't stop replaying the words Liam said to me in my head, over and over. Picking them apart and trying to figure out if he really meant this. Is this really it?

How could he toss me aside so easily with no regard for my feelings or how this might impact me?

"This sucks," I cry, taking another gulp of my wine.

Alex looks at me sadly, then pulls me to her in a hug that I apparently needed very much because the tears seem to spill even more, and my sobs increase when she does. I need my best friend, and I need someone to hold me and tell me that it will be okay.

The nanny fell in love with the family…only this time, there isn't going to be a happy ending. I lost them all, and it's left a hole inside of me that I know will never be filled. Ari and Kenendy gave me love that can never be replaced.

"Juliet, you are kind and loving, and the most compassionate person I know. If he can't see that and hold on to you like the gem that you are…then fuck him. It's his loss. You shine too brightly to let anyone steal that from you."

I nod against her chest, but say nothing. I know she's only trying to help, but right now it doesn't feel like it will ever be better. That I'll ever rid myself of the ache in my chest.

"Wanna slash his tires? I'm a sneaky bitch."

"You'd go to jail for me?"

She laughs, "Bitch, I'd do hard time. Penitentiary, orange jumpsuit style for you."

"That's true friendship, you know?"

"You know it."

THE NEWSPAPER NANNY

We sit in silence for a moment while She's All That plays in the background, and despite a broken heart, I smile at the fact that Freddy Prinz somehow manages to get the girl.

"Can I stay with you for a while? I'll have to find a new apartment. I just...I'm not ready to even think about having to do that, yet. It all feels like a bad dream—one that seems to be going on forever.

"Babe, you don't even have to ask that shit. Ride or die. That means forever, and that means you can crash in my spare bedroom when some hot shot NHL coach breaks your heart. And it also means that you bail me out of jail when I spray the word 'dick' on the side of his house."

This time, I do laugh, because my best friend is crazy, but damn, she's mine. And for the first time tonight, I feel like it might be okay...even with a broken heart.

After two bottles of Cabernet, an entire carton of chocolate ice cream, and enough tears to float Noah's Ark, I pass out in a heap with Alex. My dreams are filled with both Liam and the girls, and I toss and turn restlessly. When I wake up the next morning, my eyes are permanently red rimmed and puffy, and my heart hurts just as much as it did yesterday, if not more. Today, it feels final. I haven't heard from Liam at all, and his silence speaks volumes.

Three days pass with me wallowing in my own tears in Alex's guest room. Going to see Nana is the first place I want to be, but I have to give myself time to process everything that's happened before I see her.

The entire drive there, I can't help but find all of the places that I took the girls. The park where Ari braved the big girl swing for the first time, Antonio's where Liam kissed me like I was the last drop of water in a drought, and he couldn't survive without me.

Every place in this town has been touched by them, and now the memories in my heart are heavy as I pass them. I walk into Everwood and Andrea is standing at the reception desk, speaking with the afternoon girl. When she sees it's me, she looks up and smiles warmly.

"Juliet!"

I give her a small, meager smile, the only one I can seem to muster in this moment. My face feels puffy and stiff from the last twenty-four hours of crying.

"Hi Andrea, how are you?"

"I've been meaning to reach out to you. I just wanted to thank you for helping to organize the calendar event for the home. They raised a ton of money that will help us update so many things. Not to mention, everyone had the best time. Thank you so much. Liam and his team are just wonderful."

Her words cause the tears to well back in my eyes, and I sniffle, wiping them away, "Andrea, I didn't do much, but I'm so glad that the event was a success. Can you excuse me? I really need to see my Nana."

Great, every place I go, I seem to be surrounded by reminders of Liam. It seems like I'll never escape the pain that seems to feel bottomless. I force a smile before brushing past and all but sprinting to Nana's room.

I find her in the loveseat by the window, knitting bright yellow fabric that seems to glow in the sunlight. I want to laugh at the eccentricity of it, because it's so Nana.

The second she sees me, my face crumples, and I let out a broken sob.

"Oh, darling, come here," Nana calls.

Closing the distance between us, I curl up in the small spot on the loveseat next to her. Her frail arms wrap around me and hold me tight as the past few days come out of me in broken, ragged sobs. She does nothing but hold me tight and whisper that it will be alright, and once I'm all cried out and we're sitting in silence, I feel the first true comfort since Liam's words destroyed my heart.

"That man loves you, Juliet," Nana whispers.

"How can he love me but let me go so easily, Nana?"

I sit up and look at her, "At the first sign of struggle, he chose the route that took me away from him and the girls. He didn't even fight Nana. He just tossed me aside like I was the help. All because the tabloids want to label our relationship falsely and paint us in a bad light. Who cares what anyone else thinks?"

"Darling, I don't think that's what has happened here. I know it may seem like it, but remember things are not always as they seem. You have to put yourself in his shoes for a moment.

He's reacting to a situation he's afraid of. He's afraid to lose his job and his only way to provide for the girls. Afraid that the girls will be exposed to the media, and that's his job as a father is to protect them and shield them from things like this. Do you see that?"

"All I can see is how he discarded me, Nana. How, in just a few short minutes, he broke my heart with no regard."

"It feels like that now, darling. But, seeing things from the outside offers a new perspective. I think that you are hurt, and right now it doesn't seem like anything will make up for that hurt. I love you my sweet Juliet, always. I will always be on your side. I just think you should not be quick to condemn him for the choices he was faced with."

I sigh, "Sometimes you sound too logical, you know?"

She laughs, "Wisdom that has been earned after many years of my own heartbreak and learning from my mistakes, dear. You don't become wise without living these moments for yourself. And that's what life is all about...living and learning as we go. There is no handbook for love. There will be moments where it seems impossible, but there will always be a way. If your love is true and your heart is committed, there is nothing you can't overcome."

Her words bring fresh tears to my eyes. The truth is, I miss Liam. I miss the girls, and I miss our life together. Even though Nana is right and I think Liam is only doing what he feels like is the best for him and the girls, it doesn't make it hurt any less.

"Love finds a way, Juliet. Never forget that."

I only pray that she's right. But she didn't get this far being wrong.

CHAPTER TWENTY TWO
Liam

"You royally fucked this up, and you have to fix it." Reed says.

I drop my head into my hands for the millionth time in the past week. An entire week without Juliet, and I'm losing my damn mind. A week that has felt like a year.

The house is empty without her. Sure, me and the girls are here surrounded by their toys and every *Frozen* doll known to man, but we're missing the thing that makes our family complete. Juliet changed everything. She changed me, and I'm a fucking fool not to realize it.

But I did. The second she walked out that door, I knew I had chosen wrong. That I had fucked up, and I might not ever be able to fix it.

"You think I don't know that, Reed? I fucked up, and I don't know that she'll ever forgive me."

"Look, Liam, we've been best friends for a long fucking time. You know that I'm always going to be honest, and I'm always going to give shit to you straight. You have to stop living in the past and holding on to fear that someone is going to walk out the way that she did." He bites his lip, shaking his head. "The fact that she left was fucked. It fucked you up. I know it did. I saw it every day. But you know when it stopped? The second that Juliet walked into your life. It was no longer like you were this shell of the man you used to be. You were different. You were the guy I used to know."

I let his words sink in. Was I a different man with Juliet?

"She made you better. And fuck, I was waiting for you to pull your head out of your ass and make her yours. She's the best thing that's ever happened to you and the girls, and if you don't fight for her, you will lose her. And you will spend every day of the rest of your life wishing that you hadn't."

It was bad enough that the girls have been asking for her at least ten times a day, every single day for the past week, and I don't have answers for the questions they ask over and over.

I feel like I'm failing in protecting them, but also sacrificing what I have with Juliet in making the right choice.

What even is the right choice anymore?

My anger isn't misplaced. I didn't want to be in the public eye, but it comes with the job, and even though what Juliet and I have isn't wrong in any way...the media has done it's best to label it a scandal and taint it with hurtful headlines and a slew of lies that paint everything differently than it is.

Ari walks into the living room, clutching her doll, a tearful look in her eyes. It's way past her bedtime, but she scrambles into my arms.

"What's wrong, bug? Why aren't you sleeping?"

She sniffles, "I had a bad dream, Daddy."

I hold her tightly to me, and rock her gently. "It's okay bug, Daddy's here."

A minute passes before I hear her sniffle again, "Daddy, I miss Juliet. I miss her laying with me when the bad dreams come. She's the only one who makes it better, Daddy. Only her," she sobs.

Her words are like a sucker punch to the gut. My eyes connect with Reed, and he shrugs, shaking his head.

"I know, baby. I know."

I carry her back to her room and put her into bed then lie down with her. A few minutes later, her breathing evens out and she's asleep, but what she said still weighs on me heavily.

Juliet is our future, and I never should have let her walk out of that door. I was a fool to do so. Reed is right...if I don't fix this, if I don't go after her, then she'll slip through my fingers and I'll be left wishing every day that I hadn't let her go.

I'm not choosing between my career and the person I love.

And that much I know. I know that I love Juliet, and I know that I won't be without her based upon lies that have been plastered on headlines.

I know exactly what I need to do. The problem is...I don't know if this plan will work. But I'm sure as hell going to try. I'm going to fight for my girl.

Hours later, I'm walking through the front door of the massive building. I check in at the front desk and walk towards the back, then knock on the dark, stained wood door, waiting for an answer.

I don't deserve it, but I'm going to beg for a second chance, and God knows this is the one person who could make it happen.

Seconds later, the door swings open, and she stands on the other side with a wicked grin.

"Bout time you showed up. I was startin' to think I gave my granddaughter the wrong advice."

"Hi, Nana. Can I come in?"

She nods, holding the door open wider so I can walk through. I sit down in the arm chair across from her couch and she joins me after shutting the door closed behind us.

"I messed up. I know I did, and I don't know how to fix it. I hurt her, and I hate myself for it."

"I'll tell you the same advice I told her, Liam. Love finds a way, and you best never forget it. You're right, she is hurt. And right now, her heart is fragile and bruised. I know you love Juliet. I could see it in your eyes when I met you. The way you look at her. Both of you, crazy about each other. Neither of you had a clue, but...it wasn't my place to speak on it, but now it is."

She pats the seat next to her, and I join her on the small loveseat. Her soft, wrinkled hand covers mine, "If you love her the way that I think you do, you'll make it right. No matter the cost. You'll pay whatever price. I know it in here." She pats her heart.

"Apologizing and telling her how I feel isn't enough. I know that. I have to prove to her that what I say is true, and that I'm not going to hurt her again."

"What about your job? Have you figured out what you're going to do?"

I nod, "We're releasing a statement, at the end of the week. I'm going to tell everyone the truth. Because the truth is all I've got, and I won't lie or pretend to cover anything up. It's not who I am. I should've never asked her to walk out that door. The second she was gone, I knew I had made a mistake, but I was too much of a fool to run after her. This is me running after her, Nana. I've called her a thousand times, I've emailed. Texted. Driven by Alex's like some sort of stalker. I need you to help me make this right and get my girl."

"Darling, I knew all of this before you said it. You see, an old lady like me, I've seen enough in my lifetime to know the truth and to know when someone has a pure heart. And your heart is pure, Liam. You love those girls, and you love Juliet, and I'm gonna help you make it right. On one condition."

A grin tugs at my lips, "What's that?"

She looks over her pink glasses at me, "You organize another one of those calendar shoots for next year because boy, that sure was fun."

A laugh escapes me, real and true for the first time in over a week, and I want to hug this old woman and kiss her feet for helping me.

"Now, I have a plan."

"What do you have in mind?"

MAREN MOORE

CHAPTER TWENTY THREE
Juliet

One month later

"Would the three of you stop bickering? Good lord, I can't take it anymore!" I screech, shaking my head. Judith, Gladys and Nana have been bickering for the last thirty minutes about the janitor's last name. Judith says it's Thomas, while Gladys insists it's Richardson, and Nana is determined that it is Rockefeller.

All three of them are wrong. It's Miller.

Ask me why this matters? It doesn't. But things have been pretty quiet and boring around here and these three need some kind of entertainment.

Our Sunday morning tradition is back, and it's back with a bang. An entire month has passed since I left Liam's. During this month, I haven't spoken to him or the girls, and it still hurts as much as it did the first day. If not more now, now that it's had time to sink in and solidify that this is my new life

Back at the diner, working the graveyard shift, or any kind of shift I can get at this point, since Gary is even less Team Juliet than he was before I quit without a notice. I'm surprised he took me back, but if I had to guess my friends there had something to do with it.

Things are vastly different than they were months ago because I'm looking towards the future and determined not to dwell on the past. I re-enrolled in school and got all of my financial aid squared away. Apparently, I qualified for more grants than I knew about, and that helped with my tuition for the year. And because I'd never really spent any of my earnings from Liam, I was able to pay Nana's Everwood bill for the year, so it won't be a worry.

From the outside looking in, I guess things look like they're looking up. But every day I walk around with a dark, heavy cloud over my head. A month has passed, and I know that time is said to heal everything, but I think that's probably a crock of shit.

"Juliet?" Nana calls my name.

"Yes?"

"I asked, when your first day of class is?"

"I think two weeks from now. I have orientation next week. You know, it feels like I'm starting completely over. Even though I'll be a senior. I feel like a freshman going to school for the first time."

Nana's knitting needle moves at the speed of light as she crochets, and I watch her in awe, "You'll do great, darling, you always do."

"And, I bet they'll have cute frat guys on campus," Gladys says, joining the conversation and waggling her eyebrows.

Dating is the absolute last thing on my mind. I doubt I'll ever date again. I'm officially done putting myself out there. My heart is broken, and I doubt any amount of time is going to put it back together. Can't give myself to someone with a heart that's pieced together by bandages, after all.

"No thanks. I'm going to throw myself into my studies, pick up as many extra shifts at the diner as I can, and give myself zero time to think."

Judith rolls her eyes, "Gladys, all you do is think about men. That's why you're still single, you know. Maybe if you stopped chasing after them for a second, you'd give them the chance to chase after you."

Oh boy, here we go. I'm officially pulling out the whistle and standing referee. These ladies are sassy today. They're sassy, and I'm mopey. We're a bunch.

"Juliet, do you remember when your Pops was here, how every Sunday morning you'd sit together at the kitchen table. You eating your donuts… six glazed and six chocolate with sprinkles and him with his buttered toast."

Nana looks at me with a smile.

"Of course, I do, Nana. I miss him so much."

"Me too, darling. I think about him all the time. I was thinking about the both of you last night, and how it never failed that every Sunday when I got back from the market, I'd find you two at the kitchen table, each of you with a newspaper in hand."

I do remember those days. Even after Pops died, I still made it a habit on Sundays to read the paper, and eat donuts.

"He would always pass me the comics while he looked at the

classifieds." I laugh, "God, I remember, I would ask him, 'Pops... whatcha looking for in there, anyway?' And he'd always answer the same...'for the things that need to find me'."

Nana and I look at each other, and her eyes twinkle with amusement.

"That man was something, wasn't he? I was feeling a bit nostalgic last night, missing him and all. I picked up a paper. It's over there, if you wanna read it."

My eyes follow hers to the thick Sunday paper lying on the table. I don't hesitate to get up and walk over to it, skipping the front page, since that's not what I generally read it for anyway, and heading straight for Pops' favorite section.

The classifieds.

I grin, and look back at Nana, "You know...maybe there's something in here that needs to find me. Nana. Isn't that what the universe does? Fate and all that."

Nana nods, "You never know darling."

Gladys and Judith continue their bickering discussion on the food that's being served this week, and I just shake my head and walk back to my chair, classifieds in hand.

My eyes scan the paper and there's the usual. Lawn care, babysitter, tax person. Until I reach the bottom.

A gasp escapes my lips, and I sit up, board straight in the chair.

Oh. My. God.

I slap my hand over my mouth as tears well in my eyes. How could he have possibly known?

There on the page reads:

Nanny Needed:
Not just any nanny. One that goes by the name of Juliet.

THE NEWSPAPER NANNY

And scratch the nanny part.
We just need Juliet.
I'm sorry.
I look over at Nana, who's smiling smugly.
"Did you have something to do with this?" I ask.
She shrugs, "Whatever do you mean, darling?"
I hand her the paper and point to the spot I'm talking about. She laughs when she reads the entry and thrusts the paper back at me.

"Juliet, can you get me something to drink sweetheart? God, my throat is so scratchy," Gladys asks me before turning back to Judith.

"Uh yes, sure Gladys."

My eyes scan the ad again, and I shake my head. I can't believe he did this.

I set it down on the table to go to the vending machine, and when I open the door, I realize how quiet it is.

Hmm, weird...I don't think I've ever heard this place this quiet.

Wait, where is everyone? I look down the hallway and turn around and look the other way and it's completely deserted.

Did I miss something?

I shrug and walk through the hallway towards the main room to the vending machine. When I enter the main room, it's completely empty...except for Liam. Surrounded by hundreds of tea light candles.

I'm so shocked, I'm completely speechless. All I can do is cover my mouth while I begin to cry. My eyes lock with his, and God, it physically hurts how handsome he is. His strong, sharp jaw, chiseled to perfection. He's wearing a dark polo with dark jeans, and his hair is pushed back like he styled it. The thing I notice most? The pain in his eyes. It matches my own.

"Liam," I whisper quietly, taking the smallest of steps toward him.

"I know I'm probably the last person that you want to see right now, and I deserve that. I deserve all your anger, and all your hurt. Give me five minutes, Juliet. Just five minutes. Please."

I nod.

My foolish heart races in my chest, ready to jump at any given moment for him.

He steps closer until he's only a few feet in front of me before he speaks, "For the past five years, I've been a dad. That's it. I wasn't anything else anymore. I wasn't a hockey player, I wasn't a fiancé, I wasn't anything but Ari and Kennedy's dad. Then, their mom walked out. Kennedy was barely two months old." He pauses, rubbing his chest like the memory causes him physical pain, "Not only was I devastated that someone I thought I loved walked out without a backward glance, but now I was a single parent to the two most perfect little girls in the world, without a clue about how to raise kids. Especially alone."

His eyes are filled with pain. He's tense, and tight, and so much like the man I first met.

"I was scared. I'm man enough to admit that. I was fucking terrified. Terrified that I would fail at being their father. Terrified that I was going to fuck this up somehow, someway. I was...scared that my life would be different. It was a selfish thought, and one that I swore to myself I'd never think again. Because I was all these girls had. Me. Their mother abandoned them, and I'm the only one they had left. From that point on, nothing else mattered. It was me and my girls. I knew in my heart that, no matter what it took, I was going to do it."

Somehow, during his admission, we've come together closer. Not quite touching, but only a breath apart. I can tell his hands itch to reach out, but he doesn't. He keeps the space dividing us while he speaks.

"For the past five years, these girls have been the center of my world. I've been walking around missing something, but until you almost broke my nose at that diner, I didn't know what. And even then, I didn't know that *you* were what I was missing. You're the piece that is missing from our family, Juliet. And I know I made a mistake. I know I made the wrong choice. But you have to understand that, in the moment, given the options I had, I thought I was making the right decision for my girls. I thought that, given the choice, I was making the right one, just like I always have." He looks down at me through thick lashes, and I can see the steady rise and fall of his chest as he breathes, "I'm not asking for you to take me back. I know I don't deserve the right to waltz back into your life and expect to get you back with my apology. But I just want your forgiveness. For hurting you. For making the wrong choice. I'm sorry it took me so long to come here and make this right. I was just trying to protect everyone from what happened. I was worrying too much about my head and not following my heart. You're my heart, Juliet. You."

"Liam..." I start, but emotion clogs my throat.

"The girls miss you. I miss you. Fuck, I miss you so much that it hurts. Right here." He puts his fist over his chest, "You're the missing piece, Juliet. The only woman I know who can turn my house into a castle full of princesses and knights. The only one who can chase away their nightmares, soothe the fear in their hearts, and love them the way I can't. Because that's the thing Juliet...I've spent the last three and a half years trying to love them enough for both parents, but the truth is, all along, what they needed was you. All along, I needed you. I love you, Juliet. All of you. All the quirky, weird parts. Even the fact that you hate my food and reject any type of healthy eating. "

This time, the tears do fall, and a broken sob escapes my lips at his admission. I let out a teary laugh. Of course he would mention the cardboard that he calls food. And God, I miss my girls so much, the ache inside of me intensifies just at the mention of them.

"I want to show you something." He reaches into his back pocket and pulls out a folded piece of white paper. He opens it, and turns it around to show me.

On the paper is a drawing that looks to have been made by Ari. It's her, Kennedy, Liam...and me. Holding hands in front of a house with the title "My Family" on the front with her signature backwards. My tears fall onto the paper as I begin to really cry, so much love in my heart, it feels as if it may burst.

"I found this next to Ari's bed a few nights ago, and I knew with more certainty than ever that you're the person who makes our family complete. And one day...even if it's not now, I hope that you'll come home. Because that's what it is when you're there. A home. Our home."

His words make my tears come harder, and another sob leaves my chest, only this time it's one of happiness.

I never held it against Liam for trying to protect the girls and shield them from the media, and as time went on, I understood it more. Over the past month, I've seen how cruel and hurtful these sites can be. Absolutely hateful and vile. And it's something I hope that he can always protect the girls from. I just wish that he would've let us work together or asked for time to sort things out.

"I forgive you," I whisper.

His eyes widen. I'm sure the last thing he expected me to say is that I forgive him, but I've done a lot of soul searching in the past month, and I've realized through Nana, Gladys, and Judith that life is short. It doesn't mean that I'm not hurt, and that Liam didn't have a lot to prove, but I forgive him...

The truth is, I want my girls back, and I want Liam back more than anything, and for him to go to my Nana to set this up and do it in a way that was special to me and Pops. It's the most romantic thing I've ever seen.

"Juliet, I just...I want—"

"Liam?" I interrupt.

"What?"

"Shut up and kiss me."

And he does. In the middle of Everwood Manor nursing home, surrounded by hundreds of battery-operated tea light candles, with a pic the girls made of our family still clutched in his hand.

All because of a classified ad in the Sunday paper. DaddyISONanny.

"Aren't you glad you posted that ad?"

"You have no idea." And then...he kisses me breathless.

THE END

EPILOGUE
Juliet

Three months later

"Sugar free ice cream? Seriously, Liam." I groan, and toss the container back into the freezer with more oomph than intended.

Liam laughs, "Babe, you know this is the sugar free zone."

He's sitting at the island in the kitchen working on his laptop, watching me have a small fit over the fact that everything in this house is organic. Healthy. Gross.

"I can't take it anymore. This is a house of torture. Sometimes, a girl just needs some sugar and some unhealthy, super fatty ice cream."

Liam's eyes widen, "Wait, like should I go to the store right now and get some or…" He trails off.

"Yes, that's a great idea. Can you get some Oreos while you're at it?"

"Only if you hide them in my office."

Yes! See, there are ways around the gluten free, dairy free, non-GM), sugar free rules that he has set in place. It helps that I bribe him with some super hot sex, too. That always works.

"I'll run by the store after dance practice. Starts at four, right?"

"Yes. And it's Daddy-Daughter week, which means you better wear comfortable shoes."

It's been three months since the day Liam poured his heart out at Everwood. One blissful, ridiculously sappy month of happiness since I moved back in. Three months of officially being Liam's girlfriend.

And in those three months, so much has changed. After everything that happened with THE Puck Bunny and the nightmare of being Chicago's scandalous headlining couple, Liam decided to resign as the Avalanche's head coach. Since it was his first year coaching in the NHL, his contract was only for a year, a trial period, so he and the Avalanche parted ways.

Another hard decision that he struggled immensely with. He loves his players, he loves hockey, and he loves coaching. But he didn't love the drama that came with it, and the fact that he had to miss so much time with the girls. Not to mention the media...The last thing he wanted was for the girls to be thrust into the spotlight, so ultimately, even though it was a hard decision, he made the right one.

After he quit, he drove us crazy for the first two weeks. Seriously, I think it was the true test of our relationship. Being cooped up together for weeks with no end in sight. Until an old friend reached out and mentioned that the local high school has an open position. A hockey coaching position.

It was almost like fate, the way that it fell into his lap. He starts next week, and even though he's got first day jitters, he's excited for a new chapter in our story. One that allows him to be home every single night with the girls, and one that doesn't have reporters camping outside of our house.

It still feels kind of strange to call it our house, and honestly, sometimes I have to pinch myself that this is real. That this is my family.

That every single day I get to spend with these girls is mine, and they aren't going anywhere.

Liam and I have fallen into a comfortable routine that's become our "normal", and each day we learn more and more about each other.

Which means each day I fall more and more in love with him.

He's the most caring, kind-hearted, still grumpy man, I've ever met. And I'm sure that there is nothing he won't do for his three girls.

Like stop at the store and get me a container of sugar just because I'm on my period and I need to stuff my face with carbs.

He drops a kiss to my lips that's meant to be quick but it turns molten, quickly. The man is insatiable and can't seem to keep his hands off of me. Not that I'm complaining because I'm just as crazy about him.

"Juju?" Kennedy says, causing Liam and I to break apart quickly. While the girls know that I'm Daddy's girlfriend...they don't quite understand what that means. Lately, Kennedy has been calling me JuJu, and every time she does, my heart melts into a puddle.

"Yes, sweet girl?" I smile. Her blonde curls are going a thousand different directions.

"Can I put my le-o-tard on yet?"

The girls have a recital coming up soon, and both Kennedy and Ari have insisted on wearing their leotard at least six hours of the day, causing me to have to purchase a whole new leotard because they are wearing out the one they need for dance. Yesterday, I found Ari in her bed clutching Princess Sparkles, still in her tap shoes and pink leotard.

It's the cutest thing I've ever seen.

"Hmmm...I dunno. What do you think, Daddy? Should you practice with the girls before tonight?" I look at Liam, who just shakes his head.

"Juliet..." Liam says in a warning tone. He is so nervous for tonight, and it makes me giggle. It's just a group of little girls and their parents.

"Ken, go ahead and get the leotard and Ari. It's time to dance." I grin, and Liam shakes his head.

"The stuff I do for you girls."

"You love us. And I. Love. You," I tease, walking over to him and lacing my hands behind his neck then pulling him to me. His lips meet mine, and soon his tongue teases the seam of my lips. The movement sends a shiver down my spine, and his hands travel lower and lower until his big hands cup my ass.

He leans down again, kissing a path down my neck before whispering, "Never more than me."

That's his saying, and every day he proves it.

EPILOGUE
Liam

Six months later

Today marks the first day of the rest of our lives. I've been waiting for months for it. Dreaming about this *very* moment.

Finally, it's here.

And...I'm nervous.

Probably more nervous than I've ever been in my entire life and I've stood in the middle of *sold out* arenas of thirty-five thousand people. Yet, standing under this archway, waiting, my palms are sweaty and my heart is pounding inside my chest.

This is the moment that changes everything.

The music begins, and the sound of the violins is hauntingly soft and beautiful. The guests rise from their seats, and everyone turns to face the back.

To watch the love of my life walk down the aisle to me.

Today, I'm going to marry the woman of my dreams in front of all of our family and friends. Juliet is going to be my wife. And I have never been more sure of anything in all of my life. Before

Juliet, I was only half a man. When she walked into our lives, she changed me. Made me better. Taught me things I never knew I needed to learn.

The crowd murmurs the second she comes into view, standing at the end of the aisle. The breath leaves my lung in a gasp. Even though I've waited for this moment for months, it doesn't sink in until I see Juliet standing there in her wedding dress.

God, she's breathtaking.

The dress is everything I've pictured, and even more than I've imagined. Strapless and cinched at the waist to show off her curves, the lace bodice hugs her perfect body. Best of all? It's her mother's dress. Nana kept it for her all these years, and when she'd told Juliet, Juliet had burst into tears and sobbed for an hour straight. I thought I knew pain until I saw her break down that day.

Her dress isn't expensive. It's not from a name brand designer, like some women want on their wedding day, but it's a piece of her mother that she's able to have here with her.

For the first time in years, as long as I can even remember, I'm crying.

There's no greater gift on Earth, aside from my children, than Juliet becoming my wife and making our family whole. We're going to fill our home with love, laughter, and happiness. The thought causes the sting behind my eyes to intensify.

I realize now that, before Juliet, I had been a lost man living as just a shell of who I could have been—and I'd been completely oblivious to the fact. All I'd done was throw myself into my work and taking care of the girls, and because of that, my happiness had been on the back burner. I hadn't allowed myself to even think of what it would be like to be with anyone again...and then, Juliet had taken my life by storm.

She's the best thing that has ever happened to me and the girls—I know that without doubt or question.

The wedding march plays, and my beautiful girl walks towards me. My eyes never leave hers as she clutches onto her Nana for dear life, and the two of them make their way up the aisle. Her bright eyes are filled with tears, as are mine. I'll never forget how it feels standing here surrounded by our families and friends. How gorgeous she is in that dress. The amount of love I feel for her.

Finally, she stands before me looking more beautiful than I've ever seen her, and God, I've never loved her more.

"Who gives this woman away?" the priest asks.

"I do, young man," Nana asserts. Sassy as ever. Not only do we get Juliet, we get her Nana too. The girls adore her, and she keeps me on my toes.

Juliet looks at her with tears in her eyes and pulls her in for a hug.

"I love you, Nana," she whispers. So low that only Nana and I can hear.

"I love you more, darling."

Nana gives me Juliet's hand, and then she moves to stand next to my girls, who are off to the side, next to the rest of Juliet's bridesmaids. We decided to skip flower girls, since Ari let us know quickly that she would much prefer to be by Juliet's side. Who could argue with that?

I give them both a quick grin and wink, and they wave at me before Juliet places her shaking hand in mine, and I help her up onto the altar. Together, we walk up to stand in front of the priest, and Juliet lets out a watery giggle when I swipe away a tear that's fallen. I don't even give a shit that I've cried in front of a hundred and fifty of our family and friends. When the priest opens his book, Juliet turns around and hands her bouquet off to Alex, then turns back to face me.

It feels surreal that the moment I've spent obsessing over, planning, and praying for is finally here.

I grab both of Juliet's hands in mine and squeeze gently. Soon, I am going to get to kiss my *wife,* and I'm counting down the seconds. The priest begins the ceremony, and I almost don't even hear him speak. All I can do is stare at Juliet and try not to pull her to me to kiss her breathless. Her eyes are locked on mine, filled with tears that spill over the brim.

The minister clears his throat quietly, "Liam, you may recite your vows."

I have a piece of folded paper in my pocket with my vows messily scrawled upon it. It's a page of chaos, filled with scratch outs and mistakes, and as worried as I've been about having to recite these vows in front of everyone…I have not a single ounce of nerves as I look into Juliet's eyes.

All I feel is relief that I can finally marry the woman I love.

"I prepared for this day for months. Wrote down the things I love about you, the traits that I cherish, the things that you don't seem to notice, but I do. But every time I thought my vows were ready, I found more to add. They're in my pocket now, but I don't think they're good enough. Juliet, you taught me what love is. You make me a man I can be proud of, not only for myself, but for my girls. Our girls."

Her face crumples, and she begins to cry, but I continue on, "I promise to love you every single day of this life and into the next. I promise to love you, to cherish you, to support and encourage you, to worship you, to protect you, and to provide for you. For as long as I live. You are my soulmate and my best friend."

Juliet is crying so hard, her shoulders shake. I want to pull her into my arms and show her how deep my love runs. To make sure the only tears she cries because of me are happy ones.

"Juliet, you may recite your vows now."

She exhales a deep breath to try and stop the tears, and I squeeze her hand reassuringly. I understand, without her even having to speak. It's one of the most emotional days of my life.

"Liam." Her chin wobbles slightly, "I have never met a man like you. So compassionate, kind, and selfless. You give everything you have for us, and you never complain. You sacrifice everything for our happiness. That's what I want for our marriage. I promise to sacrifice for you, to love you, even in the moments you can't love yourself. To be your voice of reason, and to be your strength during the times when you're depleted. I promise to love you unconditionally and without hesitation, for as long as we live."

Fuck, I'm overwhelmed with love. I can't believe I'm lucky enough to call this woman mine.

The rings are passed in a blur, as I can only focus on how beautiful she is and how fucking lucky I am to have her. I slide her ring on her finger, a sparkling carat of diamond that she insisted was too much when we got it to match her engagement ring. Then, she does the same.

"By the power vested in me, I now pronounce you Mr. and Mrs. Cartright! You may kiss your bride."

I don't waste a second before I pull her to me and kiss her like it's the very first time. And...in some way, it is. It's the first kiss with her as my wife and partner. The first time that she has my last name.

I kiss her until she's breathless and fisting her tiny hands in my tux, and the crowd begins to cat call and whoop. They are our friends and family, after all. I'm not surprised.

Finally, I pull my lips from hers, and she looks up at me through thick lashes with a hazy look in her eyes.

"I can't wait to strip you out of that dress, wife."

I grin and hold her hand up with mine in triumph for the crowd as we step down from the altar and walk down the aisle. We hardly make it halfway down before both of the girls come barreling towards us and latch on to us both.

Juliet just throws her head back and laughs, and now, more than ever...I know that I made the best decision of my life by breaking the rules.

* * *

After countless dances, toasts, and conversations with every guest here, I'm fucking exhausted. I'm on my third beer of the night, and Juliet is tucked into my lap laughing at something Sophia, Hayes' wife says. They flew from Seattle for the wedding, and damn, I am glad. I hadn't realized how much I missed the guy until I got to see him again. He's only been here twice in the past couple of years with the family.

"This one never stops, I'm telling you. The other day, I found her *inside* of the toilet bowl. Feet first. I asked her what she was doing, and she told me, and I quote, "playing in da puddle.""

"She is lovely, Sophia," Juliet coos. Rook is on the dance floor with the girls, holding hands and giggling while they dance. I'm not even going to mention the fact that my chest gets a bit tight seeing them with her. I imagine a tiny version of Juliet walking around, and I suddenly want it to be a reality. Ari and Kennedy will be the best big sisters.

"Liam?" Hayes asks, pulling me from my thoughts. Dangerous thoughts.

"Yeah, sorry, zoned out watching the girls."

He laughs, "I get it man; they grow so fast. I feel like just yesterday I was reading baby books and waiting for Rook to arrive. It seems like time has passed so quickly—you don't even have time to blink."

"You're right. I swear every day the girls grow more and more, and I'm stuck wondering where it all went—when the time passed us by."

I take another pull of my beer, which is getting warmer by the second. I guess I should get us both a new drink. It looks like we'll be here for a while.

"Babe, I'm gonna go grab another beer. You want something?"

"Something fruity, please," she says.

"Sophia, can I get you anything? I'm gonna run to the bar and get drinks."

Sophia pauses, then looks at Hayes with wide eyes. Hayes just laughs out loud and pulls her in for a quick kiss on her lips.

Uh, did I miss something?

"Don't tell anyone, but Sophia is pregnant."

Juliet squeals excitedly, then hops off my lap and pulls Sophia in for a hug.

"Wow, congratulations guys. How far along are you?" I ask.

"About nine weeks. We're waiting until sixteen to announce. I had a miscarriage last year, and we just want to be sure everything is going to be okay."

I nod, "I completely understand."

The girls go back to chatting about babies, and Hayes and I just look at each other. Something about nipple shields and Kegels.

"That's our cue." He stands and picks up his cup from the table before leaning down and kissing Sophia on the cheek.

I do the same to Juliet before we exit baby talk and head towards the bar.

"Holy shit, dude, another one? Are you hoping for a boy?" I ask.

He shrugs, "Don't care. As long as the baby and Sophia are healthy, that's all that matters."

We get to the bar and watch the girls dance while we wait for our drinks.

"Did you ever think this would be our lives? Married with kids? You out of the NHL?" Hayes asks.

"Never, but damn, I'm glad it is."

Just as the bartender slides our drinks towards us, there's a loud crash, and I glance up to immediately see Briggs and a random guy I've never seen before standing to the side of the dance floor in a heated altercation. It looks like he may work for the venue, judging by the tuxedo he's wearing.

"Shit," I curse, tossing my cup onto the bar and taking off towards Briggs. Hayes follows behind me.

The two of them are chest to chest, and Briggs looks absolutely fucking murderous and unhinged, which is a bad thing when you're a professional hockey player.

"Fuck you." The guy pushes Briggs' chest hard, sending him back a few inches.

Briggs laughs, shaking his head, as if he can't believe the guy.

Instead of responding, he rears back and clocks the guy square in the face. Then, all hell breaks loose.

The guy staggers backwards before charging towards Briggs, knocking him off his feet and into the speaker to the right of the stage, which comes crashing down with a deafening impact. It sparks, and electricity flies as it smashes to pieces.

Shit, that's probably thousands of dollars' worth of equipment. What the fuck is happening right now?

Suddenly, Reed comes barreling out of nowhere towards Hayes and me. His shirt is untucked, and he looks like he was just fucking in a closet…and he probably was. Asshole.

"Fucking Christ, what did I miss?" he pants.

Before I can answer him, Briggs punches the strange man again, this time so hard I hear the sound of bone cracking.

Shit. He probably just broke the guy's nose.

Hayes, Reed and I sprint over and somehow pull the two of them apart before they kill each other. I'm holding Briggs' arms behind his back while blood pours from a gash on his temple.

"What the fuck is going on here?" Hayes barks, trying to restrain the guy Briggs is fighting with.

Briggs breaks free from my hold and straightens his shirt before wiping away the blood from his nose.

"This motherfucker is fucking my wife." The guy clutches his bloody nose and spits at Briggs, who's smirking wickedly.

Wait until THE Puck Bunny gets a hold of this….

ALSO BY MAREN MOORE

If you enjoyed Liam and Juliet's book ... pick up a copy of The Enemy Trap and find out more about Hayes and Sophia! You can read FREE with Kindle Unlimited!

WANT A SNEAK PEEK OF THE NHL'S HOTTEST PLAYER? TURN THE PAGE!

BLURB

Hayes Davis is America's sweetheart, the #1 hockey player in the country, and my fake fiancé.
Simple, right? It would be, if my betrothed were anyone else.

But it turns out America's sweetheart is arrogant, selfish, and a guy I have no intentions of letting break my heart again.

It was never supposed to happen.
But then one night changes everything.

Now, he's not only my pretend fiancé but my very real baby daddy.

How can two people who hate each other pull off the lie of a lifetime while figuring out how to raise a child together?

Everything between us was supposed to be fake, but I'm not pretending anymore.

MAREN MOORE

CHAPTER ONE
Sophia

It seems fitting that I'm ringing in the dreaded big "three-oh" wine drunk on my couch in granny panties and a semi fashionable muumuu. Honestly, if that isn't a birds-eye view of my life, then I don't know what is.

I'm not just a little drunk—I'm a lotta drunk. Like, call your ex and cry on the phone, professing your love for him—even though he cheated on you with your cousin—kind of drunk. Trust me, I hope I forget it by the time morning rolls around.

Highly, highly unlikely.

"Soph, are you listening?" my best friend Holly asks. She's sitting on the arm of my hot pink loveseat, engrossed in the subpar job she's doing of painting her toes candy apple red.

"Umm, no. Sorry, I was reliving the word vomit that just spewed from my mouth," I groan, dropping my head into my hands. This is not how I envisioned the whole "death to my twenties" party. But that's what happens when you're the last of your single friends. Everyone's married and has kids, and I'll forever be stuck being the cool aunt.

"Tell me again why I thought it would be a good idea to call him? This is going to suck a lot more when I'm hungover and semi clear-headed."

Holly shrugs. "I have no clue why you do half the shit you do, Soph. But...I said, Scott and I made a sex schedule. You know, with Brady teething and Gracie in dance, we really wanted to nail down a time." She grins, "Get it, nail? No, but seriously, how boring and predictable is my life that we have to *schedule* sex. I've officially reached my peak. It's only downhill from here."

"At least you have someone to have sex with and who *wants* to have sex with you."

She finally looks up from her toes and rolls her eyes, "Yes, sixty seconds of missionary and a faked orgasm is honestly something to look forward to."

Okay, she had a point. Still, I'd take a fake orgasm over none at all.

"Ugh, if you'd stop dating guys like Horndog Harry, this wouldn't be a problem." Her tone softens when she sees my expression, a mixture of hurt and regret, "I just hate to see you get hurt over and over by the same types of guys—scared of commitment and couldn't keep his dick in his pants if his life depended on it. Honestly, I don't know what the appeal is with him. You are definitely a ten, and he's like…a three, at best."

"It's not like I purposefully attract assholes, Hol! Apparently, I have a sign on my forehead that says "Please fuck me up." And I'm a solid seven, not a ten."

She rolls her eyes and stands abruptly, setting down the nail polish on my second-hand coffee table and stomping over to where I sit dejectedly on the arm of the couch. At five-eight, she towers over me. Her dark hair is always ten kinds of hot mess, but she pulls it off flawlessly. Holly is the only person I know who could have six days of unwashed hair, dark bags under her eyes, be wearing the same shirt as yesterday, and *still* look like a supermodel straight off the cover of Vogue. It's ridiculously unfair.

"Listen, enough of this sad bullshit. It's your birthday—we're celebrating, not crying into our beers."

"We're drinking wine..." I squint at her, trying to figure out where she's going with this.

"Whatever. You get it. Oh! Wait," she snaps her fingers, "I've got an idea. I know exactly what you need to cheer you up, and it'll be a stepping stone in the path of getting over HH and under someone else."

Here we go.

I drain my wine in one long gulp that seems to go on forever. My head spins as I swallow down the alcohol, but screw it, I'm in. In like Flynn...

She disappears into my room and comes back moments later holding the box of photos I have stashed under my bed that I wasn't even aware she knew about.

"You hussy, how did you even know about those?"

Holly rolls her eyes, "Because you're a sentimental bitch. But, no longer! We're burning this shit, and you're going to enjoy every single second of it. Goodbye to the little dick, shitty cheater of a fiancé, and hello to a brand new Sophia St. James. You're hot, single, and a solid nine."

She smirks, holding out the box and shaking it back and forth with a shimmy, as if to entice me.

What could it hurt? Maybe it'll help me let go of some of the anger I've been holding in. Lord knows I'm drunk enough to forget it in the morning.

"Fine."

I take the box from her and remove the lid. Maybe she's right; maybe it *is* time to let go of the past and move forward. Harry doesn't deserve me, and he obviously deserves my slut/homewrecking whore of a cousin. Those two are a match made in heaven. If anything, my cousin did me a favor.

"I need something harder for this. Jose, my darling, come to me," I sing-song, dancing over to the fridge.

Don't judge me. I'm going to drown my sorrow in the only man who will never break my heart.

This conversation is making me think too much about my sad, boring life. I'm stuck in the same town I grew up in: same people, same faces, same places.

Broke. Thirty. And single... Probably *forever.*

I had every reason to cry into my beer. Wine. Bottle of tequila. Whatever.

"Alright, I've decided," I tell Holly as she's rifling through my junk drawer for a lighter. "One more night of feeling sorry for myself, and then I'm going to put my big girl panties on, go back to the foundation, ask for my job back, apologize for my momentary lapse in judgment, and grow up. I mean, I'm *thirty,* " I whisper, like it's a secret I want no one to hear.

You see, I might have fallen off the deep end a tiny, minuscule amount when I found out I was being cheated on—I quit my job and wallowed on the couch for two weeks straight until Holly came over, fumigated my apartment, and made me shower.

It's not that I hate my job per se, but I feel stuck. Like I'm never going to be anything more than I am right now.

The boring job, the cheating fiancé, the backstabbing friends. Turning thirty is really making me open my eyes and see the bigger picture.

Okay, so it's only been like three hours, but still. I'm a changed woman.

"Got it! Let's go." She thrusts the lighter at me and grabs my hand, pulling me out the backdoor, even though I'm in a muumuu that barely covers my ass, "Wait, I want pictures of this as you *literally* send the old you up in flames. Like a phoenix rising from the fucking ashes, Soph."

Jesus, why did I agree to this? She is entirely too excited to light shit on fire.

Together, we light the photos and watch the memories blaze. The fire crackles and pops as it destroys a part of my life I'm not all that sorry to see go. Holly's right...I do feel lighter. Maybe it's the fact that I know this box is no longer going to be stuffed under my bed, waiting for me to pull the photos out and relive the memories over and over again. Or, maybe it's the fact that HH is a douchebag, and deep down I've always known it—I just never wanted to admit it. Catching him with Emily wasn't surprising, at least not now, after the fact. I should've seen the signs.

I should've realized that I was a ten and he was a six, at best.

And that's not just my man Jose talking.

"To stupid assholes who cheat and break our hearts, only to make us stronger." Holly raises the bottle of tequila and takes a sip, her face scrunching in distaste as it burns going down.

"You're married Hol. Happily, remember?" I laugh, snatching the bottle from her.

"This is about you, not me." Linking her arm in mine, she drags me back towards the house. "Now that you've let go of the past, it's time to move forward. We're setting you up with a dating profile and finding you Mr. Right. We'll think of a good bio that screams, "Crazy, but not crazy enough to slash your tires." Guys love crazy bitches. Trust me."

"Uh, no. Absolutely not."

"Really? What happened to the brave, bad ass, solid ten Sophia that just burned every memory of her piece of shit ex? Go take a shower; you've got ashes in your hair. Symbolic, I'm telling ya."

Half a bottle of tequila and a lot of tears later, my still delicate, broken heart lay in tatters on the floor. Add in a shower, more tears, and another signature muumuu, snuggled on the couch with my best friend, and it's a birthday I'll never forget.

The beginning of a new chapter in the messy book of my life.

"Oh, hell," Holly breathes, looking at her phone like it's grown two heads.

"What?"

She flips the phone around, showing me the screen.

I groan.

On the screen is the very person I despise more than HH, and that's saying a lot. Hayes Davis.

Of course, it's another gossip magazine and another scandal. The guy got himself in more shit than a Kardashian.

"You have got to be kidding me. Does he *want* to destroy his career? Is being a rich professional hockey player not enough for him? Gross. I mean, not that I keep up with him or anything, but he's on the cover of a different magazine every week with a new scandal in hand."

Holly gives me a knowing smile. "You know, he was voted Hollywood's Most Eligible Bachelor this year."

"Gross. Hope they had a spot for his enormous ego too."

"Yep. He called Scott last week to talk to him about it. Those two gossip on the phone more than we do."

I gag, sticking my finger down my throat for dramatic effect.

"Out of every guy in the world, they chose him. Didn't their mamas teach them that looks are deceiving?"

She rolls her eyes, "You two are ridiculous. Neither of you have moved on since high school."

"Well, that's because...because he's...Hayes Davis! Arrogant. Egotistical. Vain as they come. Ringing a bell? He *is* Scott's best friend, and for whatever reason, your kids' godfather. You should be well aware of how vile he is."

"Well, unfortunately, the world seems to disagree. Introducing Mr. Hollywood's Most Eligible Bachelor." She grins.

Hayes Davis. America's sweetheart, and my number one enemy. Yep, even over HH and his cheating pencil dick.

I'd rather use cardboard tampons than spend another second of my time talking about him.

"No, but really, you guys would be so cute together, Soph. Maybe it's time you stop fake hating him and let Scott and I hook you up. He's hot—you can't deny it. Remember, we're leaving the past in the past?"

"Hol! He's your husband's best friend." I cry, my eyes wide.

Shrugging, she looks back at her computer, "So? He *is* on *People's* Sexiest Men Alive list, so it's merely an observation of fact."

"Too bad they don't account for how big egos are when they choose them, or Hayes would be screwed. I think he's making up for what he lacks in dick size."

"Sophia St. James, you are so hot for him. Stop lying."

Another gag, and I'm five seconds from puking on my Goodwill couch. Hot pink velvet and puke do not mix. I can think of at least ten torture activities I'd prefer over being in the same room with Hayes. Thankfully, even though he's Scott's best friend, he's busy warming every puck bunny's bed from here to Seattle, so I rarely have to be subjected to seeing him.

Only for the kids' birthdays and the occasional holiday, which is more than enough for me. The less the better.

I didn't like to give Scott shit about it since we were all adults, and I really should be over the whole number one enemy from childhood thing, but...I'm a huge grudge holder, so I'm not getting over this anytime soon.

It doesn't help that the few times Hayes *does* come home, he flaunts his money and a new bimbo on his arm. Not that I would ever—and I mean ever—admit it out loud, but he *was* ridiculously attractive, to the point that I wanted to punch him in the balls just for being so insanely handsome.

No one should be that perfect on the outside and so ugly on the inside. Life can be so unfair sometimes.

"I'd rather you run me over with your car than touch Hayes."

"Dramatic. Whatever. It was just an idea. It's time to put yourself back out there, Soph. It's been over six months since HH. Can we please put you on the dating site? Just give it a shot. If it sucks, you can delete your profile."

"Dating sites are gross. A giant waste of time. I already tried it, and it was a shitshow. Everyone pretends to be someone they aren't just to match with someone. Remember that time I met the guy who brought his mother? He paid more attention to her than me."

She squints her nose when she remembers that date. "Okay, true. But that was just one. You can't let one ruin it for them all."

"Okay...What about the guy who sucked his thumb...at thirty? Oh, or what about the one who recorded all our conversations so he could replay them later?"

"Alright. Fine. No dating sites. But, at least give your number to that guy from yoga. He was super hot."

I shake my head. "And he also likes the same guys that I do, Hol. Stop playing matchmaker. I'm fine being alone. Actually, I'm thriving being single, free, and happy with myself. Really."

"Whatever you say, Soph."

Okay, I was lying. We both knew it. I hated being alone. I preferred to be in a relationship, however comfortable it was, even if sex was scheduled. I'd choose that over waking up each morning alone.

"Fine. I was lying."

"I know."

"One dating site. One. And not the Singles in Seattle one. That one was full of weirdos. Oh, what about this one?" I point to Tinder.

"Yes!" She squeals, clicking on the signup button. "You're going to meet the man of your dreams, just watch. When you least expect it, Mr. Perfect is going to sweep in and sweep you off your feet."

Famous last words, if there ever were any.

WANT TO FIND OUT WHAT HAPPENS NEXT? PICK UP YOUR COPY OF THE ENEMY TRAP NOW AVAILABLE ON AMAZON!

ABOUT THE AUTHOR

Maren Moore is the alter ego of R. Holmes. Author of dark, angsty and forbidden romance. Desperate to let the lighter, fluffier side reign free, she created Maren.
You can always expect alphas and HEA's that are dripping of sweetness from her.

MAREN MOORE

ACKNOWLEDGMENTS

Everyone always asks me what is my favorite part about writing a book, and while there are so many things that I love about publishing, this part is my favorite.

Giving the credit where it's really due. Because without these people, I wouldn't be who I am. I wouldn't be able to publish or write, and I can never thank them enough for the sacrifices they've made.

To my best friend in the world, Holly Renee. I love you. Words are useless when it comes to how I feel. Soul sisters for life.

To Jac, I could write an entire book about how much you mean to me, but I just hope you know that I love you unconditionally and I cherish you.

Katie, this book would not exist without you. Period. That is a fact. You held my hand, and pushed me when I thought I couldn't finish. I owe everything to you. I love you.

To my author friends who continually support, encourage, and offer guidance…. I treasure each and every one of you. You are a light in my life. All of the **Savage Queens** (literally all of you lol!) Trilina Pucci, Meagan Brandy, Giana Darling, CoraLee June,

Alley Ciz, SJ Sylvis, Julia Wolf, Shantel Tessier, Samantha Lind, Eliah Greenwood, Amanda Richardson and so many more. Love you girls.

To Alex, Haley and Jan for being my alphas and betas. Your advice is so critical to my writing. I couldn't do it without you. I love you each SO much.

To my amazing publicist Amanda who I really don't deserve. Thank you for all of your hard work and your friendship. I CANNOT LIVE WITHOUT YOU AMANDA. Okay? Love you.

To my street team, and to my Facebook group Give Me Moore. Thank you for all of the hard work that you do. You share, repost, comment and hype my books and it is so very much appreciated.

And as always, thank you to the readers and bloggers who pick this up and take a chance on me. Whether you loved or hated it, the fact that you took the chance means everything. Without you, our world wouldn't turn.

THE NEWSPAPER NANNY

CPSIA information can be obtained
at www.ICGtesting.com
Printed in the USA
BVHW041045140223
658482BV00006B/190